HARLEY'S HEART

by

Magnolia "Maggie" Rivers

Dream big!

Maggie Rivers

Published by

Freeman Group, L.L.C.
Des Moines, IA

HARLEY'S HEART
by Magnolia "Maggie" Rivers

Published by Freeman Group, L.L.C.
Des Moines, IA

First Printing: October 1, 2018

Print:
ISBN-13/EAN-13: 978-1-943793-10-5

E-book:
ISBN-13/EAN-13: 978-1-943793-11-2

Cover design: E.J. Whitmer

Printed in the United States of America

Dedication

To: All the kids I grew up with. You know who
you are.

Thanks for all the fond memories from my
childhood. It wouldn't have been the same
without all of you. From climbing trees
(and some of us falling out of them) to
swimming in mudholes, we had a blast.
We grew up in the best of times!

You were the greatest group of friends to
grow up with and I cherish you all!

Go Wildcats! And, Roll Tide, Roll!

Love,

Maggie

Dedication
(continued)

To my son, J.D.

As always, you are the "wind beneath my wings".

From the first moment I saw you, you became the air I breathe. Without you, my world would cease to exist.

I love ya, babe! You are my hero.

I am so very, very proud of you!

To my daughter-in-law, Sheila

Thanks for making him happy. I'm so glad he found you!

In loving memory of my mama,
Vaudeen Freeman
(July 14, 1924 – November 5, 2009)
Mama, you were the best mom ever! I still miss you daily.

In loving memory of my daddy,
Bueford Freeman
(August 2, 1924 – May 16, 2018)
Daddy, you were the best daddy a girl could ever have. I miss you daily!

In loving memory of my friend and fellow author,
Bob W. Dunbar
(Oct 11, 1949-Mar 4, 2018)

A Vietnam Veteran, Bob was the author of two historical novels. The first, _The Holy Sabbath Morning: a Novel of the Alamo_, tells the story of the famous battle from the points of view of participants on both sides. The later one, _To Fame's Proud Cliff_, deals with the relationship between two of the most remarkable men in American History: Sam Houston and Andrew Jackson. (Proceeds from the sale of Bob's books now go into a college fund for his two grandsons.)

Bob was editing a contemporary novel called "_Between the Winds: the Odyssey of the Walkin' Dude_" at the time of his death. It is now being finished by his daughter. Bob was loved by all who knew him and will forever be missed by our writing group. Walk on "Walkin' Dude" walk on!

I shall forever miss your Million Dollar Wattage!

THANKS TO

Jeff L. Makemson
Supervising Wildlife Biologist – District III
Alabama Division of Wildlife and
*   Freshwater Fisheries*
8211 McFarland Blvd. West
Northport, AL 35476
Office (205) 339-5716
Mobile (334) 467-5368
Fax (205) 333-2900
Jeff.Makemson@dcnr.alabama.gov
www.outdooralabama.gov.

A special thanks to Jeff Makemson for his assistance in creating "Tiny," the wood bison. All discrepancies in the behavioral characteristics of "Tiny" compared to those of real wood bisons, are totally those of my creative imagination.

Wood bison are the larger of the two subspecies of modern American bison. Adult males are approximately 6 feet tall at the shoulder, 10 feet long, and weigh more than 2,000 pounds. "Tiny" is not tiny at all!

Thank you, Jeff!

Jennifer Wright
Chick-fil-A
2652 Old Denton Rd
Carrollton, TX
A thank you to Jennifer Wright for allowing me to use the photo she took of The Missing Man Table at the Chick-fil-A in Carrollton, TX. A fitting tribute to all my military brothers and sisters who never returned. Thank you, Jennifer!

THANKS TO
(continued)

Nicole Smith
Chick-fil-A
2652 Old Denton Rd
Carrollton, TX
A huge thank you to Nicole Smith, the lady on duty at Chick-fil-A when I contacted them to find out who had taken that particular photo of The Missing Man Table. Thanks for your assistance in answering my questions and putting me in contact with Ms. Wright. Your help was invaluable!

HARLEY'S HEART

By

Magnolia "Maggie" Rivers

CHAPTER ONE

Deputy Dakota James Dalton sat at a small table covered with a red and white checkered plastic tablecloth, watching the biker riding down Main Street into his small Alabama town. Something about this biker drew Dakota's attention. A Harley rider dressed all in black leather and helmet, kept Cody from seeing the color of the man's skin. The biker rode in slowly and pulled into a spot in front of the cafe where Cody sat looking out the front window.

"Can I get you something else, Cody?" asked Katy Hughes, breaking into his concentration as she stood beside his table holding a steaming pot of coffee.

"Thanks, Katy, but I'm good," he replied, his eyes never leaving the rider.

Cody watched as the biker removed leather gloves and stuffed them into his leather jacket.

He must be sweating in that get up.

July in Shady Rivers was hot and humid. What was it that bothered him about this man? Picking up his cup of coffee and taking a sip, Cody continued to watch as the biker took a moment to look around. Still something about this particular biker just did not seem right. Instinctively, Cody reached down and touched the gun he carried in the holster on his hip. Shady Rivers might not be a very big town but it was his town and he aimed to keep the riff-raff at bay. He continued to watch and wait. All his senses functioning at high alert.

The biker finally reached up and unsnapped the black helmet, lifting it up and off as long curly blonde hair fell out.

"Well, I'll be damned," Cody whispered, "a girl."

CHAPTER TWO

Cody watched as the woman took a few steps forward, glanced back over both shoulders, then entered the cafe and sauntered up to the end of the counter. Swinging her leg over the stool, she sat down as Katy hurried over with her order pad in hand.

"Hi, what can I get you?" Katy asked.

"Coffee to start with."

"Coffee coming right up," said Katy as she walked over and grabbed the pot and a cup before returning to the counter. Setting the cup down in front of the woman, she poured a steaming cup.

"Nice looking little town you have here," said the woman as she glanced around, taking in the small cafe's atmosphere. Her gaze landed on a bulletin board at the right of the counter with the words 'Pass it Forward' in big red letters at the top.

"I like it," Katy replied.

"You live here long?"

"All my life," said Katy as she turned and placed the coffee pot back on its burner.

"How many people you got here?"

"Last count we had I think it was a hundred and four."

"I like small towns. People tend to know everybody."

"That they do. Sometimes that's good but other times, everybody knows your business. Can I get you anything else?"

"Maybe a cheeseburger and fries."

"A cheeseburger and fries coming right up," said Katy.

"Could you add a fried egg on it?"

"A cheeseburger with a fried egg on top then," said Katy as she smiled and walked toward the order window.

"You seem to be awfully interested in our quiet little town. Why is that?" asked Cody as he took a seat on the stool next to the woman.

Cody watched as the woman's gaze traveled from his face all the way down to his boots and back to his eyes.

"I didn't invite you into this conversation, so I really don't see where it's any of your business, Barney Fife," she said as she turned back to her cup of coffee and took a sip.

"Well, Harley," said Cody, "as I see it, everything in this town is my business so you just might want to get back on that Harley you rode in on and keep right on going, unless you want to explain to me why you're so interested in our little slice of heaven here."

"Well, Barney, since when is making conversation with a waitress against the law?"

"Conversation isn't against the law in these parts but it's the curiosity that killed the cat, so to speak," said Cody.

Katy sat a plate in front of the woman.

"Here you are," said Katy. "One cheeseburger, complete with fried egg on top and fries. You want a refill on the coffee?"

"Actually, I'd like a Coke and some ketchup for the fries, please."

"Coming right up," said Katy as she retrieved the ketchup from under the counter, sat it in front of the woman and headed toward the Coke machine.

"So you're a ketchup with fries person," said Cody. "What's with the fried egg thing?"

"What's with the inquisition?" asked the woman as she squeezed a mound of ketchup onto her plate.

"Just making conversation. What's your name?"

"I think you called me Harley."

"Yeah, but what's your real name?"

"Listen, Deputy Dawg, I haven't done anything but ride into town looking for a place to grab some food and maybe have a little interesting conversation to go with it. Now if that's against the law..."

"Sorry, I may have come across a little strong, but in this business, you can't be too careful. You're just a little out of the ordinary for our little town."

"Well, I'm really sorry if I don't fit your stereotypical small-town woman, whatever that is, but with me, it's what you see is what you get. So, if you don't like what you see, I consider that your problem, not mine. Now, while I'd really like to carry on a useless conversation with you, I have what looks like some great food to eat, if you don't mind." She turned and picked up her cheeseburger and took a bite.

7

"Not a problem at all. Enjoy your lunch," said Cody as he stood up from the counter stool. "If you need anything while you're visiting, the Sheriff's Office is to the left and on the corner there. Feel free to stop in anytime."

"I'll keep that in mind," she said as she picked up a French fry with her fingers and dipped it into the mound of ketchup, before taking a bite.

"You have a nice day, now," he said as he placed his hat on his head and tipped it at Harley. "See ya later, Katy," he called out as he turned and walked out of the cafe.

CHAPTER THREE

"That guy always a jerk," asked Harley.

Katy chuckled.

"No, most of the time he's really a nice guy. Give you the shirt off his back if he thought you needed it. He must just be having a bad day or something."

"Well, you know what? I may just have to stay over a day or two just to rub him the wrong way. Give Barney Fife something to do." She laughed as she picked up her Coke and took a sip.

"Well, girl, you just do that. Somebody needs to shake him up a bit," said Katy as she began to wipe the counter. "So, where you headed?"

"Nowhere in particular. Just looking for a change of scenery. Had an Aunt on my mother's side who use to live here."

"'Zat right? What was her name?"

"Matilda Swanson. People called her Tilly. Don't suppose you knew her?"

"Of course, I knew her. I think at one time or another, she taught every kid in town. When I was a little girl, my mother and Tilly were good friends. Always brought me her home-made cookies. They were delicious."

"That's awesome. I never expected to find anybody who actually remembered her living here."

"Everybody in town knew Tilly."

"What kind of a lady was she?"

"Oh, you know, a grandmotherly type. Kind of plump, but not too plump. Gray hair put up in a bun on the back of her head. After she retired from teaching, she always had an apron on over her dress. She loved to bake. Always had warm cookies for us kids on the weekends when we'd be out playing."

"Actually," said Harley as she dipped another French fry into the mound of ketchup on her plate, "I don't remember much about her myself. She always sent me birthday cards with a few dollars tucked inside and something at Christmas. I never lived close enough to any of my relatives to actually get to know them. Always wanted to but never had the chance."

"Where you from?"

"Everywhere. Dad was a military man. We moved a lot and I mean a lot. Name's Bridgette by the way. Most people just call me Bri. But don't tell that to Deputy Dawg. He can just call me Harley," she said as she laughed.

"Well, I'm Katy and it's nice to meet you, Bri."

"It's nice to meet you, too."

"Ya know, I think people are happier when they have roots. Some place they can call home with some good memories," said Katy.

"I wouldn't know what that feels like. Always wanted to though."

10

Katy heard the longing in Bri's voice.

"Well, you just hang around this town for a bit and you'll get that feeling in no time at all."

"I may just do that. Have to be around for a few days anyway. I've got to see what shape Aunt Tilly's house is in. It's mine now and I'm planning on selling it. So, if you know anybody who's looking, send 'em my way, would ya?"

"Sure thing. You do know it's rented out right now, don't you?"

"Yeah, the real estate company told me that. Say, what's with the board over there?" asked Bri nodding in that direction.

"Oh, that's our Pay It Forward board. People round here like to help each other out when they can. So they'll buy an extra cup of coffee or something and put a card up there with whatever it is they've bought on it and then when somebody comes in and needs it, they take a card off and get whatever's on the card."

"Kinda like paying for the guy behind you in the drive-thru lane at a McDonald's or something. I like that. People helping each other instead of always trying to scam one another. No wonder Aunt Tilly stayed here. Nice bunch of people. You open for supper?"

"Yep, three meals a day, plus dessert and coffee anytime."

"Now that sounds wonderful to me. You do cheesecake?"

"Best in town. I get it from Becky's Bakery over yonder," said Katy as she nodded in the bakery's direction. "She's been making cheesecake since before I was born."

"Then I'll be back," said Harley as she stood up and tossed her money on the counter.

"Great. See ya later then," said Katy as she smiled.

"Yep, see ya later," said Harley as she turned and walked out of the cafe.

CHAPTER FOUR

"Hey, Spence," said Cody as he walked into the Sheriff's office.

"Cody," acknowledged Sheriff Spencer Cartwright looking up from his paperwork.

"Thought I'd stop in before I headed home to get some shut eye before my shift. Anything going on?"

"Nope. Same ol', same ol'," said Spence.

"Well, you should have been over at Katy's a few minutes ago."

"Why's that?" asked Spence as he tossed the last piece of paper into his outbox.

"You should have seen what I just saw," said Cody.

"Not ol' Tiny?"

"Nope, much better than that."

"Okay, I'll bite. What'd you see?"

"A biker babe."

"You watching too much television?"

"No. I mean she came riding up on her Harley. Right up Main Street. I kept looking at her to start with 'cause you couldn't tell if she was a guy or gal."

"Well, if you couldn't tell what sex she was she couldn't have been too much of a looker," said Spence as he sat his coffee cup back on his desk and leaned back in his chair, propping his feet up on the desk.

"Oh, no, she's a hottie alright. Got a mouth on her, too. She came riding up Main on a humdinger of a Harley. Couldn't see an ounce of skin. Just black leather and this black helmet. I kept looking. Thought at first it was a guy, but somethin' just didn't seem quite right, ya know. Kept on bugging me. Then when she stopped and took off her helmet and all that blonde hair fell out. Yep, that's one hot looking biker babe. Would've made any man salivate for sure."

"Over the babe or the bike?" Spence chuckled.

"Oh, the bike was a humdinger alright. But the babe, haven't seen anything that good looking around these parts in a coon's age."

"Cool your jets, bucko. She just passing through?"

"Don't know. She was asking Katy a lot of questions about our little town though."

"No harm in that. Probably just making conversation."

"That's what she said, but I got the feeling there was more to it," said Cody. "She seemed a bit wary to me. Looking over her shoulder kind of thing on the way in and then sat at the counter with her back to the sidewall. Little things like that."

"Well, tell you what," said Spence as he removed his feet from the desk and sat up. "You keep an eye on the hottie and if she does any jaywalking we can arrest her and throw her in the cell back there and—"

"Hell no! That'd be like putting a damn cougar back there. She'd rip the place apart."

"Sounds like this girl is just what you need, my boy. She got you tied in knots already and she hasn't been here a whole day yet," said Spence as he got up from his chair. "I'm heading over to talk to Katy for a bit. Guess our mystery bandit came back into town last night. Took some stuff from her place."

"Again? Seems like whoever the culprit is hits her place more than anybody else's."

"Looking for food I suspect. Probably just some homeless guy passing through. He'll hang around for a bit and then move on. But, just in case it's something else, I'm gonna go have a talk with her."

"Okay, I'm outta here then. See ya later tonight."

"Yeah, go get some sleep and I'll see ya later," said Spence as he grabbed his hat from the rack beside the door and headed out.

CHAPTER FIVE

"Hey Katy, girl," said Spence as he opened the door and walked into the cafe.

"Hey, Spence," said Katy. "You want the usual?"

"Yep. No use in changing now," he said as he took a seat at the counter. "Place seems a little deserted today."

"You're just later than normal," said Katy as she turned and yelled back to the order window. "The usual for Spence, Gus."

"The usual coming right up," replied Gus.

"I was just beginning to wonder if you were out chasing Tiny or something," said Katy.

"Actually I haven't seen Ol' Tiny in a few days. You?"

"Yeah, he was by here this morning for his usual," Katy replied.

"Figures. That ol' boy knows a good fried apple pie when he tastes it."

"He sure beats anything I've ever seen. I sure would like to know where he came from."

"Well, you just don't see too many bison wandering around the south these days. I expect someday he'll just wander out like he wandered in."

"I still think he had to come from a circus or something like that. I mean, him being nothing but a big baby and all," said Katy.

"Could be. Could be. So, what're you missing this time?"

"Usual kind of stuff. A couple of my biggest cans of pork 'n beans, a salt-cured ham, and a couple of my apple pies. He or she, as the case may be, sure has a sweet tooth."

"Anything else? Money?" asked Spence.

"Nope. I haven't emptied the tip jar in a few nights and it had about thirty dollars in it, but he didn't take it."

"Interesting."

"Oh, and a can of coffee. Regular, not the decaf."

"That it?" said Spence as he folded his notebook and stuck it back into his shirt pocket.

"Yep, I think so. Now, let me get your hamburger and fries," said Katy as she turned and headed back to the order window.

* * *

Harley parked her bike in front of the address she'd been given for Aunt Tilly's house. There were no cars parked outside so she assumed no one was home.

Bob McAllister, the real estate agent over in Tuscaloosa, had explained about the tenant living there and the fact he had six more months on his lease. She was hoping to talk him into either buying the place or moving out before that six months was up. She needed money and a quick sale of the house would keep her going until her Dad's estate could be settled.

Plus, she intended to stay in the upstairs until she could get it sold. Mr. McAllister had told her there was a sort of fire escape stairway leading up to the second floor from the outside. She decided she could use that and, since her dad had stored all her Aunt's things on the second and third floors, those floors had not been included in the lease with the tenant. And, with only eighty-four dollars left before she'd have to stand in the soup lines, she needed a place to stay. She wasn't sure how this tenant would cotton to that idea either.

Hearing a vehicle approaching up the long tree-lined driveway, she turned toward the sound. Harley watched as a truck pulled up into the unattached building she'd thought was a barn. At least that's what it looked like, complete with hay loft. Guess the tenant used it as a garage for his sporty pick 'em up truck. She had to giggle to herself. She'd heard just about every country song there was on the radio while she was traveling around the country.

She stood waiting for the man to walk back out of the building.

"Well, I'll be damned," said Harley the moment she caught sight of the man. He had yet to look in her direction. She watched as he pulled the barn's doors closed and lowered the latch before he turned to walk toward the house and her.

He stopped in mid-stride.

"What the hell are you doing here?" asked Cody.

"I might ask you the same thing," Harley replied as she leaned against her bike.

"I live here. What's your excuse?" he asked as he continued to walk toward her.

"So you're my tenant" Harley said as she watched the expression on his face turn from surprise to something around the 'oh shit' marker. Harley grinned.

"Don't tell me. Let me guess. You own this place." Cody stood a few feet away letting the information sink in. He wasn't too pleased about it either. "I knew there was more to your story than what you were letting on back there at Katy's," he said.

"I'm not in the habit of discussing my business with strangers."

"Well, I've got a lease that says I can live here for six more months. So if you'll excuse me..."

"Yeah, about that lease. See, I need to talk to you about that. I'm selling the place. Thought I'd play nice and let you have the first chance to buy it since you're already living here and all."

"Buy it? Hell, you gonna repair it first?"

"What's to repair?"

"I'm thinking a lot. Don't think the real estate company who's supposed to look after the place apparently, has been doing too good a job. Roof leaks. Floor boards on the porch have rotted in places. I can't get into the second or third floor to see the damage there. It's off limits and locked up tighter 'n a drum."

"Well, how about if you just forget about the lease and find some other place to live. I can sell it then and we can both forget about it."

"Hell no. I'm just fine here for another six months."

"Okay, then. I'll just get my saddle bags off my bike and head on in to the second floor. I'm going to be living here for the next six months."

CHAPTER SIX

"To hell you are! I've got the place leased. Or did you forget that little item."

"No, I haven't forgotten at all. But, if you'll check your lease, it's only for the first floor. The second and third floors are mine to do with as I please. And right now, I please to go inside and get settled in."

Harley lifted her saddle bags and headed for the front porch with Cody in hot pursuit. She wanted to laugh out loud but kept her mind on walking and did her best to keep her shoulders from shaking with laughter.

"Well, then, you're not stepping foot on the first floor. That's mine. So just how you plan on getting in and out of your part of the house?" Cody stopped on the front step and waited for her reply.

"Well, Barney Fife, there's a fire escape on the side of the house, if you haven't noticed. I'll be using that."

"You'll break your neck. Thing'll probably fall first step you take on it."

"Guess we'll see," said Harley as she turned and walked in the direction of the side porch.

Sticking her head around the corner, she caught sight of the rickety fire escape stairs. Didn't look like they'd hold up a kitten, much less a full-grown woman. But with only eighty-four dollars left to her name, she had no choice but to try.

Walking around to the bottom of the stairs, Harley braced her hand against the railing. The stairs were only wide enough for one person to climb with the steps themselves only about four inches deep. Harley stood there looking up at the top of the stairway to the small outside doorway on the second floor.

"Listen, wait a minute," said Cody, "I'm not going to stand here and let you try to climb that deathtrap. Not until you get it fixed at least. Come on, I'll let you use the hall stairs for a couple of days. But just until you can get this damn thing fixed."

Cody turned and headed back around to the front. Reaching up on top of the front door frame, he pulled down a key.

"That's a little dangerous, don't you think?" said Harley as Cody stuck the key in the lock, opened the door and put the key back onto its resting place.

"Maybe where you come from," said Cody, "but folks around here trust one another."

"That so?"

"Yep, we're just plain country folks around here. None of them highfallutin' city people ever come nosing round our little town. Well, except during the holidays when the Christmas Artisan Festival is going on. Rest of the time, people around here are just decent country folks."

"Must be nice."

"Stairs are at the end of that hall," said Cody as he stepped aside and pointed down the hallway.

"Thanks. I'll get those stairs fixed as soon as I can. Is there a hardware store in town?" she asked glancing around at what she could see of the old house as she walked passed Cody. For some strange reason it felt like she imagined coming home might feel. It was a nice, warm feeling somewhere deep down inside.

"Wright's is two doors down from Katy's where you had lunch."

"Oh, okay. I'll get some screws and tighten the stairs up tomorrow then," she said as she headed toward the doorway at the end of the hall.

"It's gonna take more than a few screws to fix that staircase," said Cody as he laughed. "Some of the brackets have already rusted clean into."

"Oh. Didn't think about that. Listen, I'm rather short on cash at the moment. Do you think you can fix it? If so, I could take it off your rent and it might help us both out."

"Yeah, I could do that, I guess. I'll take a closer look at it tomorrow and see what all I'll need. Right now, though, I have to get some shut eye. I work tonight."

"Okay, that's fine with me," said Harley as she turned and unlocked the two deadbolts with the key the realtor had given her and headed up the stairs, pulling the door closed behind her.

Climbing the stairs, she inhaled the musky aroma of years gone by. It was the closest she'd ever been to real family. For a brief moment, she stood still listening, waiting, although she wasn't quite sure what she was waiting for.

25

Continuing to climb, she reached the top and stepped out into what would have been a sitting room had it not been so piled high with old furniture and boxes.

"Lord, love a duck." Harley stood glancing around at the mess. This was going to take some time. From the looks of it, her tenant's lease would run out long before she got to the bottom of the mess.

"First things first. A path to the bed for tonight and a path to the bathroom for now," she said as she shoved at the boxes in her path. A shower would be nice after riding all day. Especially in hot weather.

Pulling her saddlebag off her shoulder, she tossed it on top of one of the boxes and made her way toward what she assumed might be the bathroom.

She managed to shove the smaller boxes aside enough to get her legs in between as she made her way through the maze. Finally, reaching the door, she opened it and found the bathroom minus any boxes.

"Well, thank you, karma for the small things," she said as she stripped off the leather jacket and tossed it on the floor. Quickly removing the remainder of her clothing, she stretched, hoping to relieve some of the day's tension from her body.

Naked, she reached over and drew back the shower curtain. Her gaze caught movement on the bathtub floor. The scream that left her lips, as she hopped onto the commode seat slinging her hands furiously in the air, was blood curdling.

CHAPTER SEVEN

Cody heard the panicked scream from above. Jumping from the shower, he grabbed at a towel as he ran from the bathroom, stopping just long enough at the nightstand beside his bed to grab his gun before heading down the hallway to the stairs which led to Harley's apartment.

Damn, he should have checked the place out before he allowed her to go in there by herself. No telling who was up there. There'd been those reports of stuff missing around town.

Cody reached for the doorknob. It opened. Thank goodness she'd forgotten to lock it when she went up.

The screaming continued. He could hear thumping. All he could think was hurry, get there, man, before someone slits her throat.

Reaching the door, he swung it open, gun drawn. His gaze fell upon Harley with her hands flinging in the air, trying to keep herself balanced on the commode seat as she jumped from foot to foot. She was naked. Totally naked. Pulling his eyes away from her body, he followed her gaze to the bathtub, his gun following the same path.

Nothing.

"What? What?" he yelled at Harley.

"Kill it, kill it!" she screamed pointing toward the bathtub.

"What? What?" Cody yelled again.

"There, there! Kill it, kill it!" Harley continued her commode dance.

Cody caught movement out of the corner of his eye. It was black and crawly. A spider. The woman was screaming bloody murder over a spider. A goldang spider. He'd risked life and limb for a goldang spider.

The screaming continued.

"Okay, okay," he said, "calm down. It's not going to hurt you. Thing's probably just as scared of you as you are of it."

"Don't care! Kill it! Just kill it!"

"Alright, alright. I'll take care of it. Just calm down and relax." Cody looked around and ripped a corner off one of the boxes closest to the door. He leaned over the bathtub and laid it in front of the spider.

"What are you doing?" asked Harley as she stopped the jumping and reverted to dancing from one foot to the other.

"Come on little guy," he coaxed. "Get on the cardboard before it's too late," he said as he placed his fingers behind the spider and drummed on the floor of the tub.

"Stop that. Just kill the thing." Harley yelled, still flinging her hands in the air.

"Look," said Cody, "how 'bout if you just look the other way for a few minutes and let me take care of the little guy. Then we can talk."

"Hurry, just do something and get that thing out of my sight."

"There, he's on the cardboard. Now, close your eyes and I'll walk by and head outside with him."

"Oh, geez, don't let it touch me," Harley pleaded.

"Hang on, it'll be gone in a minute," said Cody as he walked passed Harley trying hard to keep his mind off her naked body. He felt a drop of water trickle down his temple from his wet hair.

Taking the cardboard-riding spider over to a window, he raised it and deposited the spider on the outside windowsill.

"If I were you, little guy, I'd be sure and stay out of her sight from now on. Take it as a warning. Next time you may not be so lucky."

Cody closed the window and walked back to Harley who was still dancing on the commode seat. For a moment he stood there and drank in the sight of her. This woman did things to him. From the first moment he laid eyes on her there'd been something about her. Something that drew him like a moth to a flame. Sirens seem to be going off in his head and his lower region stirred.

"Okay, he's gone now. You can open your eyes," said Cody as he tightened the towel around his waist.

Harley opened one eye, glancing around.

"You sure?" she asked in a whisper.

"Yep. He left to go visit relatives over in T-Town."

"T-Town?"

"Tuscaloosa. You're safe." Cody smiled as he just stood there staring for a moment. "You do realize you're naked, don't you?" he asked as he noticed the fact she was a true blonde.

"What?" Harley looked down at her bare body. "Oh hell," she screamed as she quickly crossed her arms in front of her chest, then quickly moved one hand down to cover her girlie parts.

Cody stood there enjoying the show.

"Well, you're not dressed either," she replied. "I mean, you're in a towel. A gentleman would hand me that towel," she said nodding toward one hanging on the towel rack.

Cody grinned and slowly reached down grabbing hold of the top of the towel around his waist.

"Oh no, oh no! Don't you dare!"

"Oh, anything for a lady in distress," he said as he whipped off his towel and tossed it up to her.

Harley squished her eyes shut as her hands grabbed the towel and held it up in front of her.

Cody laughed as he turned and headed back to the door leading down the stairway.

"Next time you're naked just yell. I'm sure I can take care of any problem you might have." He looked down to the lower portion of his body which stood at attention, then looked back at Harley and smiled before pulling the door closed behind himself.

Oh I just bet you could. "Not a rat's chance in hell!" she yelled back at him.

CHAPTER EIGHT

"Hey Cody," said Spence as he looked up from the paperwork he'd just finished.

"Hey, man," Cody replied as he tossed his hat on the wall peg just inside the office door.

"You look a little worse for wear. Last I knew you were headed home to get some sleep," said Spence as he turned and filed his paperwork in the file cabinet behind him.

"Yeah, but I had a spider crisis to handle and after that I didn't get much sleep."

Spence laughed.

"A spider crisis? Didn't know you were afraid of spiders," said Spence.

"Hell, it wasn't me. It was the girl on the Harley."

Spence turned around.

"What'd you do? Don't tell me you went chasing after her instead of going home."

"Not exactly. Turns out she's my landlady."

"Landlady?"

"Yeah, she's related to Tilly Swanson and owns my place."

"You kiddin' me?" asked Spence as he stood and walked around his desk.

"Nope. She's here to get the place in shape. Wants to sell it."

"You thinkin' of buying it?"

"Hadn't really given it any thought. I mean, I like the place and all, but always thought about living out in the country, ya know."

"Yeah, I know exactly what you mean," said Spence as he opened his desk drawer, removed his gun and holster and strapped it around his hips.

"Always did want to watch the deer roaming around from my back porch, ya know."

"Awesome sight isn't it?'

"Only thing that might be better is watching a passel of kids playing on the lawn on a Sunday afternoon."

"Sounds like it'd make a good song," laughed Spence.

"Yeah, I think it already has," Cody chuckled.

"So she's gonna sell the ol' place?"

"That's what she says anyway."

"Well, who knows, maybe somebody'll change her mind for her?" said Spence as he opened the office door, walked out and closed it behind him. He had his own lovely lady to go home to and that's just where he was heading.

* * *

The morning sun stretched lazily across the town square as Bubba Jones slunk quietly around the corner trying not to be seen which was downright difficult for a man of his physique. With biceps the size of watermelons and covered with tattoos, his six foot four, three-hundred-pound frame was hard to disguise.

"Miss Katy, Miss Katy," He called out as he rounded the corner of Katy's Kitchen.

"Oh, hey, Bubba honey," said Katy as she glanced around, from unlocking her cafe door, and saw Bubba headed toward her with Van Gogh clutched to his chest. She knew he was partial to the old cat ever since he rescued it from a coyote. Since it was missing an ear from the encounter, Bubba had named it Van Gogh.

"Miss Katy, I'm sorry to bother you and if you don't want me around, well, after you know," Bubba dropped his gaze to the sidewalk. It had been six months since the incident and he knew people were still talking about him. He felt really bad about beating up on Jonette. Normally, when it came time to fight, he used brains over brawn, but Jonette had floored him by surprise.

Katy thought he looked like a kid who'd gotten caught raiding the cookie jar.

"Bubba, honey, you listen to me. I'm not one to judge other people. Lord knows I got enough trouble of my own without takin' on everybody else's. You're welcome here anytime you want. And if anybody gives you a hard time in my cafe, they'll answer to me for it."

"I'm much obliged to you, Miss Katy," he said as a small smile crept around the corner of his mouth.

"Now you come on in and it'll just take me a minute to get opened up this morning, but I'm sure Gus is already in the back, and I can get you some breakfast ordered," said Katy as she pushed open the door, flipped on the front lights and stepped inside.

"I don't need no breakfast for me, Miss Katy, but Van Gogh here would be much obliged for a bowl of milk."

"Well, Van Gogh can certainly get a bowl of milk anytime he needs," Katy smiled, her blue eyes twinkling. "Come on in. You want a cup of coffee or something?" she asked over her shoulder.

"Naw, much obliged though. I had mine before I left my place this morning," said Bubba as he half sat on the counter stool. "Just didn't have any milk for Vanny here and he's pretty partial to his milk in the mornings."

"Well, I don't blame him a bit. Here you are Van Gogh," she said as she sat a large saucer of milk onto the floor next to the counter.

Bubba sat the squirming cat down and watched as it lapped at the bowl of milk.

"I'll have to stop at Hale's on my way home this evening and get a gallon for him."

"You taking him to work with you or you want me to just let him out when he's done?" Katy asked as she flipped on the coffee maker.

"If you could just let him out, that'd be great. I can head on in to work. Don't want to be late or anything," said Bubba.

"Well, don't you worry none about Van Gogh. Me and him'll do just fine," said Katy as she leaned against the edge of the counter.

"Thank you, Miss Katy, I'm shore obliging to ya."

"Well, I'm always glad to help out a friend, Bubba, honey. Stop by anytime. You have a good day, now, ya hear."

"Thank you, ma'am. You have a good day, too. Van Gogh, you behave yourself for Miss Katy now, ya hear."

Katy watched as Bubba patted the cat's head before walking out of the cafe and heading across the town square to the garage. She noticed the forlorn slouch of his shoulders. He was hurting and in a bad way. He'd been dealt a horrible blow to his masculine ego. She only hoped he was man enough for the challenges which lay ahead and that his heart would be man enough to deal with them.

Gus stood in the kitchen doorway watching Katy talk to the cat as it drank its milk. The thing he liked about her the most was her big, kind heart. No one was ever turned away at Katy's Kitchen. Not even him. He knew, he of all people, surely didn't deserve her kindness. He only hoped that someday he'd be good enough to deserve a woman like her.

CHAPTER NINE

"Morning sugarbabes," said Dixie as she took the last chair around Flo's back table. "How's it going with you, Nadine, honey?"

"Oh, sugar, I'm grinnin' like a possum eatin' a sweet tater. Ya know that handyman I hired to fix stuff up, courtesy of ol' scumbag's credit card?"

"Yeah, he sure was a hottie," said Honey. "He can just dill my pickle anytime he wants. Lawd, but that man was a sight for sore eyes." Honey took a sip of her coffee. "You got anything to put in this?" she asked glancing up at Flo.

"Cream, sugar or both?" asked Flo.

"Baileys'd be a whole lot better," replied Honey as she laughed. "I need a good kickstarter this early in the morning. I ain't getting' no sex so may as well drown my sorrows a little".

"Girl, since when ain't you gettin' sex? Hell, I think ever' man, married or single in this town, would jump at the chance to oblige you in that department," said Stella.

"Well, that's the problem," Honey replied. "There ain't a whole lot of eligible men in this town. We need to plan us a girls' night out and

37

head over to T-town and see what's hanging around over there. Might catch us a redneck or two."

"Listen," said Nadine, "I hear tell the scumbag's been hanging around some new little thang up there in Birmingham. Maybe after we do Tuscaloosa, we should take a road trip on up to Birmingham and pay her a visit before he gets himself another one," said Nadine. "You know, I still can't believe I didn't know he had three other wives."

"And what kept the other three from finding out about you. I mean, what kept him from calling out one of his other wives' names, you know, when he was in the throes of doing the nasty with you or any one of them?"

"Maybe he did and we just weren't listening," replied Nadine. "Harvey wasn't the stud in bed he thought he was. He was more like a wham bam thank you ma'am kind of guy. Actually, you can forget the thank you ma'am part. He was asleep by that time." Nadine giggled.

"Girl, you are too much," said Honey.

"Well, I'm with Nadine. I think we should do a girls' night out and find the scumbag before he can marry another poor unsuspecting woman," said Stella.

"You know, I think I feel sorriest for that one, what was her name? You know, the one with those two little babies," said Dixie.

"Oh, you mean, Charlene," replied Nadine.

"Yeah, I mean, she's got those two little babies and that jackass couldn't even keep his pecker in his pants long enough for her to even get out of the hospital after she had the first one.

Hell, he must've climbed on her the minute they brought her out of the delivery room," said Dixie.

"Yeah, we need to do something special to him in her name. Hell, I'd be Lorena Bobbitt and just cut off his tallywacker but I don't look good in prison orange so we'll just have to find somethin' else to do to the scumbag in her honor," replied Nadine.

"Oh, oh, oh, I've got it!" squealed Dixie, "We need to humiliate him in public. I mean really humiliate him. What size shoes does he wear, Nadine, honey?"

"Size thirteen. He's got big feet. Why?"

"Well, we need a pair of stilettos that'll fit him."

"Stilettos," said Flo. "Oh, this is gonna be good. I can tell already."

CHAPTER TEN

Gertie Mae Gillespie walked out the door of Katy's Kitchen carrying the fried apple pie she'd bought for Tiny in a brown paper sack. She walked over to the park and stopped beside the large garden fountain. Removing the pie from the bag, she poked a hole in the center of it with her finger.

Looking around, she quickly took a small bottle of oil from her purse, unscrewed the lid and poured half its contents into the hole in the pie before putting the lid back on and dropping the bottle back into her purse which hung over her shoulder. She stood waiting.

With her gray hair caught up in a bun on the back of her head she could almost pass for her own mother. She was like her mother in the hair department, too. It hadn't started turning gray until she had hit seventy years old and now, two years later, it was completely gray. A nice shade of steel gray.

Holding the brown paper sack in front of her, she spied her target up ahead lumbering in her direction.

The old bison snorted when he caught sight of her. His pace increased, and it seemed to Gertie he was definitely in a hurry for his morning medicinal pie.

She knew Katy had probably already fed him one of her fried apple pies but her own pies were special. She used a very special ingredient in hers that would help the ol' guy's arthritis pain and nobody was any wiser. She knew Tiny felt better just like she did.

She'd not believed it when she'd first been told about its medicinal value, but the pain had been bad enough she would have tried anything. So, when her nephew said he had something guaranteed to help, she opted to try it. She felt so much better and so did Tiny.

Tiny stuffed his nose against the brown paper sack Gertie carried. He grunted loudly, his tongue licking at the bag.

"Hold on Big Guy," said Gertie, "Mama's gonna take care of you. I got what you need."

Reaching into the bag she pulled out the fried apple pie and held it out to Tiny.

Tiny chomped half of the pie down in the first bite and finished it off licking at Gertie's hand.

Gertie swore the animal smiled at her.

"Now, you just take it easy for a little while and let that kick in and you'll feel much better. I know how those ol' bones can hurt. That's why I use it. It's medicinal you know."

Tiny grunted and sniffed the bag as though looking for more of the treat before lumbering off to continue his morning rounds.

"Just like a man, get what you want and leave," said Gertie as she walked on through the park towards Katy's Kitchen. She sure had the munchies again this morning and Katy's was just the place to take care of that.

CHAPTER ELEVEN

Bubba finished up his day's work and waved goodbye at Joe South before heading out of the shop on his way back home. He'd put in an extra hour and really didn't feel like going home and cooking for himself, so he headed to Katy's Kitchen instead. He would stop off at Hale's to pick up milk and cat food for Van Gogh before he headed home.

"Hey Bubba, why such a hang-dog look on your face?" Katy asked as she poured him a cup of coffee.

"Been a hard day, is all."

"Bubba, honey, I've known you since we was kids and I can read you like a book. Now, let me get you something to eat and you can talk to me about what's really eatin' at you? So, what'll it be?"

"How about the meatloaf and add a side portion to go for Van Gogh."

"I swear you spoil that cat," Katy laughed. "Gus, the meatloaf for Bubba with a dab to go for Van Gogh."

"Be right up," Gus hollered back.

"Now, talk to me," said Katy propping her arms on the counter as she leaned in to listen to Bubba.

"It's just that when I left here this morning, I walked through the Square heading over to the garage for work. Me and, well, you know. We used to walk through there and sit on that there gazebo all the time. But this morning, there was some of the town ladies sitting there and when they saw me, they just started laughing."

"Oh, honey, if they were really laughing at you, I'm so sorry. But you know how ladies are. One of 'em could have just told a joke or something and you just happened to walk by at that minute."

"No, it wasn't like that. They's laughing at me."

"Well, if they were really laughing at you, then it just goes to show how small minded they are. People like that aren't worth your time. You're a better person than that."

"I don't know that Jonette would agree with you on that. I tell ya, Katy, I just lost it."

"Well, under that circumstance, I can see why you'd do that. Now, let me tell you something. The way I see this little mishap is you can do one of two things. You can forget about Jonette entirely and get on with your life from this point or, if you still have feelings for her, you can talk things out with her and see where it takes you."

"But, she was a he!"

"I know, honey, and the word here is *was* a he. Now, I'm no expert on the subject or anything like that, but the way I see it is, there are people born ever which way. I mean some are

46

born with both parts down there. They don't have a choice of which part they're going to keep. Guess the parents make that choice for them."

Leaning in a little closer, she continued, "Now what if the parents make the wrong choice. I mean, think about it. Just suppose all the other parts in that body is female yet the parents wanted a boy so they choose to take away the female part. That doesn't change the rest of the body. The brain thinks it's female and it's in charge of the rest of the body and it says hey, listen up all you cells. We're a female so act like it. And that little baby walks like a female, looks like a female, thinks like a female and everything is female except for this one body part. You can't make the rest of the body act in a certain way just because it has some junk in the trunk."

"I guess I never thought about it like that," said Bubba. "But I mean, Jonette was a guy. I mean, she had that junk and all. That just goes against everything I've ever known," said Bubba as he wiped his hand across his face.

"Well think about it from Jonette's perspective. Everything about her, everything she's ever known felt wrong. She was told she was a boy. She was dressed like a boy, given boy toys and even a boy's name but somewhere deep down inside, she knew something was wrong with that picture. She didn't know what but she just felt wrong. She wanted to play with girl things, and wanted to dress in girls' clothes but everything she'd ever been taught told her that was wrong. She had to be so confused as a child. How horrible that must have been for her. It's hard as a kid to fit in even if you weren't born

47

that way but, in her case, she never quite fit into her own body."

"Miss Katy, you are a very wise lady."

"Oh, I'm not so sure about that. It's just that if you try to walk a mile in someone else's shoes you get a better look at what makes them who they are. Ya know?"

"Order up," hollered Gus as he sat Bubba's plate in the order window.

Katy turned, grabbed the order and sat it down in front of Bubba, along with Van Gogh's packed and ready to go.

"Can I tell you something, Miss Katy, I mean, just between you and me?"

"Bubba, anything you say to me is just between you and me," said Katy as she patted his big hand with her small one.

"Is it bad if, well, you know, I mean, is it bad if," Bubba hung his head, "if you know, I mean—"

"It's okay, hon, it's me you're talkin' to, you can say it to me," Katy said as she reached over and lifted his chin, so she could look him in the eye.

"It's just that, well, it's just that—"

The bell over the door jingled as Spence walked in.

CHAPTER TWELVE

"Ladies," said Spence, nodding at Gertie Mae and Agnes as he passed their table before making his way up to the counter where Bubba sat talking with Katy.

"Hey, Spence," said Katy as she poured him a cup of coffee. "You heading home for the night?"

"Yep, just thought I'd grab a quick cup of coffee and two slices of that cheesecake to go. Abby loves that stuff."

"Can't says I blame her. Two slices of cheesecake to go, coming right up," said Katy as she poured a cup of hot coffee and set it in front of Spence before turning to grab two small go boxes.

"Bubba," said Spence, "how's it going?"

"Can't complain," replied Bubba looking down at his plate.

"What's Van Gogh up to these days?" Spence asked as he took a sip of his coffee.

"Waitin' for his supper probably," said Bubba. "I was just too tired to cook after work today. Thought I'd stop by here and grab a quick bite before heading home."

"Don't blame you there," said Spence.

"Here you are Spence," said Katy as she returned with the cheesecake packaged up and ready to go.

"Thanks, Katy," said Spence as he finished the last swallow of coffee and tossed his money on the counter before standing up.

"Tell Abby I said enjoy," said Katy.

"I'll do that," Spence replied as he turned and headed back outside.

"Now, Bubba, honey, what was it you wanted to say?" asked Katy as she refilled his coffee.

"I don't know, Miss Katy, I'm just confused is all," said Bubba as he finished the last of his meatloaf.

"I know, honey," said Katy, "you just don't know what to do about those feelings you still have for her, do you?"

"I don't know what to feel, Miss Katy. It's just so confusing. I mean, I know Jonette's a girl, now, but she's also a boy. I mean was a boy, I mean, oh, I don't know what I mean anymore," said Bubba as he pushed his plate away.

"I know, sweetie. It goes against everything yore mama taught you, don't it?"

"It does, Miss Katy, it shorly does."

"Well, sometimes, Bubba, we have to decide what's right for us. I mean sometimes things change in this old world. Things our parents never had to deal with, you know. Now, you take, for instance, when your grandma was around, I'll just bet she never thought about a person flying to the moon and back. But, now, we've already had people who've actually walked on it. Things that your grandma knew about changed and if

50

she were here today, she'd have to readjust her thinking, wouldn't you say?"

"That she would, Miss Katy, that she would," said Bubba as he spit out a laugh, "Kinda like when they discovered the world was round and not flat."

"Exactly, just like that. So the way I see this is, if you still have feelings for Jonette, you just have to readjust your thinking on this whole he/she thing."

"You know, Miss Katy, you are one smart lady."

"I don't know about smart, Bubba, but I like to look at a problem from all sides before I make a decision. Sometimes, though, we just don't see all the sides until they've been pointed out to us. I mean, we're so caught up in what we were taught that sometimes we can't see the other sides."

"Well, yore a whole lot smarter than me."

"Nope, not at all. I may be smarter in somethings, but you're smarter than me in somethings, too. I mean, I can't fix my car when something goes wrong with it and you can take any car apart and put it all back together again. So that definitely makes you smarter than me when it comes to cars. And if I remember correctly, you were reading from books by the time you were three. Heck, it took me until I was seven and then I wasn't much good at it." Katy laughed.

"I'm shore obliged to you, Miss Katy. I mean, for letting me talk to you and all," said Bubba as he stood up and handed her his ticket along with his money. "I gotta head on home and feed Van Gogh. Much obliged."

51

"You give Van Gogh a kiss from me, now, ya hear."

"I'll do that, Miss Katy, I'll shore do that."

Bubba walked out the door as Skeeter Johnson bounced through.

"Katy, darlin'," said Skeeter as he jumped up with both bare feet and squatted on the counter stool, "You got me some dinner ready?"

"Always, sweetie, always. Gus, hon, Skeeter's here," Katy yelled back to the kitchen.

"Coming right out," Gus yelled back as he sat a brown paper bag in the order window.

Katy turned around, grabbed the bag from the window and sat it on the counter in front of Skeeter.

"Here you are. Can I get you anything else?"

"That'll do me, that'll do me," said Skeeter as he fidgeted on the stool and quickly glanced around the restaurant at the rest of the patrons. "Gotta go now. Things to do."

"See ya tomorrow, Skeet," yelled Gus.

"Tomorrow, tomorrow then," said Skeeter as he leaped from the stool and scurried out the door as quickly as he had come in.

CHAPTER THIRTEEN

Cody sat behind the Sheriff's desk, his feet propped up on it, and drank the last swigs of coffee from his cup. Damn but that woman was something else. Standing on the toilet seat, jumping up and down over a spider as naked as the day she was born. Now that was a sight he thoroughly enjoyed.

Plus, she rode in on a Harley. That was enough to set his libido itching but then finding out she was his landlady and was actually going to be living right above him was the icing on the proverbial cake. He'd just have to be sure to round up some more spiders for the fun of it. Yep, that was one naked body memory he was going to enjoy reliving as often as possible.

Setting his coffee cup down on the desk, he lowered his feet to the floor, grabbed his gun from the desk drawer and stood up. He walked toward the door, grabbing his hat from the peg on the wall as he opened the door. He would make his rounds before heading over to Katy's for some supper later.

Stepping outside, he heard music floating on the air and recognized the sweet sound of

Elmer's dulcimer and Mel's banjo, too. This time of the evening, they would be sitting over in the town square picking out a little southern soul. It was sure nice living in a small southern town.

He was glad he had made that decision a few years back when he'd finally retired from the military. He'd snuck in when he was sixteen because he needed a home, and he had spent the next twenty years there. But now he was living the peaceful life he had always dreamed about when he was still a kid.

Fishing when he wanted to, nobody to answer to except for his job. And, he loved his job. Shady Rivers was not a major metropolis by any stretch of the imagination and he liked it just fine. Everybody knew everybody and that was just fine with him.

Once outside his office, he turned to his left and headed toward the Pickin' Porch and the music. Yep, the slower southern country life suited him just fine.

Cody walked along the sidewalk, stopping at the front doors of the businesses along the way, checking to be sure they were locked tight. Not that it really mattered if they were or weren't because there hadn't been a real break-in in Shady Rivers since Buddy Hollings got sent to juvenile detention years ago. He'd heard about that kid from just about every resident in Shady Rivers since he became deputy.

At least no break-ins other than whoever it was who stole food and a few necessities every few months. Cody figured that was someone just down on their luck. Never took money or anything of value. He'd been there before himself.

He knew the kind of person who would do that kind of stealing. He'd been one himself back then. He'd just been too young to help except for the food he stole and brought home. He had always felt so bad doing it but he had to feed his mom and sister as best he could.

He'd kept track of it all though and once he'd gotten his first paycheck from the Air Force, he started paying for all he'd stolen. A few dollars here and there stuffed in an envelope and mailed to the people he owed. He'd paid them all back. He often wondered about the thoughts that went through their mind when they opened the envelope and found the money.

He'd done what he had to do at the time. During those years, he took care of his women as best as any kid could. He smiled to himself knowing his mother would have been proud of him now. Looking toward the heavens he whispered, "I'm doing fine, mom. Just fine. Kiss Angel for me." Cody's hand slipped into his pants pocket and his fingers touched what he was searching for. "Tell her I still have my Barlow knife." With his other hand, he checked the door on the Sweet Strings Dulcimer Shop before he turned and crossed the street into the town square.

CHAPTER FOURTEEN

Harley sat on the gazebo railing listening to the music on the night air. She hadn't been there long before she noticed Cody coming out of the Sheriff's office. She watched him walk down the sidewalk checking to be sure doors were locked as he went. And every time she thought about him handing her his towel earlier, she couldn't help but grin. She definitely liked what she had seen.

Living above a hunky cop was not going to be easy. Especially now that she'd seen what was underneath his uniform. Visions of it standing at attention kept her awake last night and revved her motor to high alert.

She had managed to avoid him all day. Waiting until there were no sounds coming from his part of the house, she had crept down the stairs and out the front door. She headed to Katy's for some breakfast and then to Hale's for a few groceries before returning home to put the groceries away and do more unpacking of Aunt Tilly's boxes.

Now, freshly showered, she'd waited until Cody left the house for work before she had ventured out again.

She'd stopped at Katy's for a cup of coffee to go and took it with her to sit in the town square and watch the people walk by. A few had stopped and actually talked with her. Yeah, she could definitely get used to small town living. Everybody seemed friendly, always calling out hellos to everybody they knew and it seemed like everybody knew everybody.

Talking with Elmer Shelton, she'd learned a little bit more about her Aunt Tilly. Seems everybody knew her. Most either were in her classroom themselves or had kids who had been. Aunt Tilly apparently had had a good life here. This might be just the place Harley was looking for herself.

She caught sight of Cody as he glanced in her direction. She saw the look of recognition cross his face and a smile spread across his lips. She'd like to run her tongue across those lips and taste them. Quickly, she tried to push that thought back to wherever it had come from. She watched as Cody strolled across the park toward her, stopping long enough to say hello to several people here and there.

That man was one nice piece of eye-candy. Her breathing quickened as she watched the muscles in his thighs flex with each step he took. Why did this man do things to her? She was definitely not used to these types of feelings assaulting her senses. She'd had enough trouble trying to push the memory of his naked body out of her mind so she could sleep. She did not succeed last night and she was not succeeding today either.

Cody walked up to the gazebo and stood with one leg propped up on the first step.

"We meet again," he said as a smile played at the corner of his mouth.

"You're very observant, Barney," replied Harley.

Cody let his gaze wander from her hazel eyes to her rose-pink lips. He'd like to taste those lips. They looked so soft in the moonlight.

"So, tell me, Harley, what do you think of our little town so far?"

"It's a nice little town. Friendly people. I can see why Aunt Tilly stayed here."

"Yeah, I kinda like it here myself. Some nice people in this town. Give you the shirt off their back if you needed it kind of people."

"You born here?" asked Harley as she took another sip of her coffee.

"Nope. Moved here a little over three years ago."

"Why here?"

"Say, you had supper yet? I'm buying," said Cody, "We can catch up on each other's lives."

"I don't think you call it catching up if you never knew the person in the first place."

"Well, we can just pretend."

"Aren't you on duty?" said Harley as she stood up.

"Yeah, but I do get a supper break. Come on, Katy's got something good, I'm sure."

"Well, she does cook a mean cheeseburger, that's for sure," said Harley as she stepped off the gazebo.

"Then Katy's it is," said Cody as he offered her his arm. "M'Lady?"

Harley took his arm and felt the warmth from his hand as he placed it over hers. The chemistry between them sent tingles to her girlie parts. This was not going to be an easy night. The last time she'd had sex was over a year ago and may have well been non-existent for all it was worth to her. It was over with before it got started. She never saw the guy again and it was just as well. She'd found most men were into getting their own jollies without any regard to her pleasure at all. Something about Cody spoke differently to her, but she'd learned to listen to her own brain where men were concerned.

"Hey, you two," said Katy, looking up as the door jingled.

"Hey Katy," said Cody. "How about a couple of Gus' best steaks and some of Miss Becky's cheesecake for dessert?"

"You got it. How you want those steaks?"

"Harley?" asked Cody as he turned toward her.

"Make mine medium rare," said Harley.

"One medium rare, and rare for you, Cody? Sweet tea for you Cody and if I remember correctly, it was a Coke for you, Harley."

"You would be correct, but make it a sweet tea for tonight," said Harley.

"Two sweet teas it is then," replied Katy as she turned to get the drinks.

Cody steered Harley to a booth in the corner.

"So," said Cody after he had seated Harley and himself, "catch me up on all I've missed since you were born." He grinned.

60

"You haven't missed much. Military brat. Moved all the time. Aunt Tilly died. I inherited her place. That's pretty much it in a nutshell. What about you?"

"Managed to retire from the Air Force. Passing through Shady Rivers on my way to Florida. Met a lady here that first day and just never left."

"So what happened to the lady?"

"She passed away."

"Oh, I'm sorry."

"It wasn't like that at all. She was just a nice older lady. Kinda reminded me of someone."

"So you just decided to stay cause she looked like somebody you knew?"

"Here you are, two sweet teas. Steaks'll be up in a minute," said Katy as she sat the glasses down on the table and headed back toward the counter.

"No, she didn't really look like anybody I knew, just kinda reminded me of somebody."

"Oh. So, do you like living here?"

"Yeah, actually I do. It's kind of like having a family where everybody is family. Does that make sense?"

"Maybe. I've kind of gotten that same feeling since I've been here. I just couldn't put it into words," said Harley as she took a sip of her tea.

"Yeah. I like the slower pace of life here. Nobody seems to be in too big of a hurry about anything."

"Why is that?"

"Oh, I'm thinking southerners know something about life and family that people in other parts of the country just don't know about.

I mean, I think they've figured out that it's family that matters most and slowing down and just enjoying each minute as it comes. I mean, now tell me the truth. When's the last time you stopped and watched a honey bee gathering nectar on a beautiful flower blossom?"

Harley laughed. "Not since I was a kid, that's for sure."

"Well, you should."

"Here you are," said Katy as she sat plates of food on the table. "Be right back with some more tea for you," she said as she hurried off again.

"So tell me about my Aunt Tilly. Did you know her well?"

"You could say that, I guess," said Cody as he took a bite of his steak. "Ummmm, this is delicious. Not sure how Gus ended up here cooking in Katy's Kitchen with his culinary expertise but I, for one, am really glad he did. That man can cook a steak."

"This really is good," said Harley. "What in the world does he do to it?"

"That's a secret only Gus knows. He don't share his cooking secrets with nobody!"

"Well, he's got my vote on this one. I think this is the best steak I've ever eaten," said Harley as she took another bite.

"With steaks by Gus and cheesecakes by Mrs. Becky, hell, I'd have been a fool not to stay here," said Cody as he laughed.

"Well, I've already had some of Mrs. Becky's cheesecake and if I stay here much longer I'll gain too much weight to be able to ever leave."

"I think that's Tiny's problem. He's eaten too many of Katy's fried apple pies to ever leave."

"Who's Tiny?" asked Harley.

"Oh, you haven't met the town's buffalo yet?"

"The town has a buffalo?" asked Harley. She could only imagine the look of total surprise that must have crossed her face.

"Yeah, ol' Tiny. Don't worry, he won't hurt you none unless you have a fried apple pie and you don't share it with him. He takes that as a downright insult." Cody laughed.

"A buffalo."

"Yep, ol' Tiny just kind of showed up here one day. Guess he smelled some fried apple pies sitting on the windowsill over there and he just showed up and helped himself to all of them."

"You're kidding me, right?"

"Oh, I kid you not. He ate all them pies and I swear he fell in love with Katy. Makes his rounds around town every single day."

"A buffalo?"

"Yep, and one of the biggest fellows you'll ever see, I reckon'. At shoulder height I'd say he was over six feet and about a couple thousand pounds. But don't let him scare you none though. He really is a gentle giant."

"So where does he stay when he's not eating fried apple pies?"

"Oh, he wanders off in the woods at times. But he has places he likes to go for handouts and, like I said, he's a lovesick puppy when it comes to our Katy. He'll follow her anytime she's out and about. I swear you can see little red hearts floating up out of his eyes every time he looks at her. Just like in one of them cartoons you see in the paper. He's gotten partial to Mrs. Gertie Mae, too."

63

"Well, hell's bells."

Cody laughed. "Listen, I hate to eat and run in such a hurry, but I have to get back to work. Can I walk you back some place?"

"No, no, you go ahead. I'm going to just sit here a bit and drink some coffee and chat with Katy before I head back home."

"Okay, and don't forget about taking a walk and smelling some flowers and watching some bees. Slow down a little and enjoy the Southern life for a spell," said Cody as he removed his wallet from his pocket and laid money on the table for Katy. Turning, he waved at Katy before heading toward the door.

Harley watched as Cody stepped outside into the night air. She liked the back view just as much as she did the front. Maybe she should just sell Tilly's things along with the house and leave before she got herself in trouble. This man was trouble with a capital T for sure. He did things to her. Nice things. Things she could certainly enjoy if taken a little farther.

She'd have to keep her mind on business any time he was around. Strictly business. She was in trouble already.

CHAPTER FIFTEEN

"Van Gogh licked the last remains of the milk from the bowl and sat watching Bubba as he picked up the last bite of cheesecake from the paper container Katy had put it in.

"What's with you, big fella?" asked Bubba. "I gave you your dinner." Bubba raised the fork to his mouth while still eyeing the cat who continued staring at the morsel of food.

"Alright, alright," said Bubba as he lowered the fork to the cat's plate and dropped the remaining bite.

Van Gogh finished off the cheesecake before rubbing against Bubba's legs purring in contentment.

"You know, ol' man," said Bubba, "you got it easy. Cats are just cats. I mean, you don't wake up one day and decide you're a dog. You're just a cat. You's born a cat and you's just stay a cat. But now if you's a people it'd be different. You could wake up and be something else. I tell you, Vanny, it's just not easy being a people. I'm thinking I want to be a cat. It'd just be much easier."

Bubba got up from his table and picked up the cat's paper plate along with his own and tossed them in the garbage.

"Come on ol' man. I'll turn the tube on for you and we'll see if we can find you a bird show or something to watch," said Bubba as he walked into his living room and turned on the television. Van Gogh took his usual spot on the back of the couch and waited.

* * *

Spence sat with his feet propped up on the coffee table with Abby's head laying against his shoulder. Her breathing came in a steady rhythm. Spence kissed the top of her head. She gave up a lot when she married a small-town sheriff and he knew it. If it were possible to love her more for it, then he surely did.

They hadn't really planned on Abby getting pregnant so soon but it was certainly alright with him. He'd like a Spence, Jr. or even a little Abby look alike running around. He'd be happy with either as long as Abby was alright. Other women her age had successful pregnancies so she would, too. He'd just have to be sure she got plenty of rest and did what her doctor said.

Abby stirred.

"Abs, honey, let me take you to bed. You can rest better that way," said Spence as he gently brushed the hair back from her face.

"No, no, you finish watching your show. I can get myself to bed," she said as she straightened up, putting her feet down on the floor.

"I know you can, but I like putting you to bed myself. I get to help you undress that way," he laughed as he stood up and lifted her into his arms.

"Well, that's what got me in this predicament in the first place," said Abby as she smiled up at him.

"I happen to like this predicament. It looks good on you."

"You're such a sweet talker. That must have been why I married you in the first place." Abby put her arms around his neck. She placed her hand against his cheek and turned his face to hers.

Spence bent down and kissed the tip of her nose.

"I love you, Mrs. Cartwright," he said.

"And I love you, too, Mr. Cartwright."

Spence carried her to the bedroom and carefully laid her on the bed.

"Let me get your shoes off and then I'll get to the more delectable parts," he said as he wiggled his eyebrows in his best Groucho Marx imitation.

"You goof ball," said Abby laughingly.

"Yeah, but I'm your goof ball," he said as he pulled off both her tennis shoes and tossed them over his shoulder. "Now let me get those pants."

"Careful, that could get you in lots of trouble."

"I'm no stranger to trouble."

"You're such a card. Could I get a foot rub while you're at it?"

"One foot rub coming up. How about a back rub while I'm at it?"

"That would be soooooo nice."

CHAPTER SIXTEEN

"Harley heard Cody knocking on the hall door.

"Morning, sunshine," said Cody, how'd you sleep last night?

"Like a log, actually," said Harley. "I'm glad Aunt Tilly had an air conditioner in the bedroom up there. Turned that sucker on icicles, threw one of her quilts on the bed and I don't think I moved until the sun hit my face this morning."

"Anytime you need extra body heat you just let me know. I can keep you toasty all night long."

"Thank you for the offer but the quilt was just right. And there's more of them if I need," she replied with a smirk on her face.

"I'll have to see what I can do about that," said Cody as he half turned toward the front door. "Shall we?" he said as he offered up his arm.

"Lead the way," Harley replied as she stepped off the last of the stairs and stood next to him.

Cody turned and headed back down the hallway toward the front door.

Harley followed close behind watching his butt move in the tight jeans he was wearing. One thing she loved was a nice tight butt with jeans that showed it off well. Too many guys missed a great opportunity by wearing baggy jeans hanging down below their butt cheeks and showing their underwear. That was disgusting as far as she was concerned. She had yet to meet any woman who professed to love a man's butt in saggy underwear with their jeans falling off.

No, she liked tight jeans and she knew exactly what was underneath Cody's. Thoughts of that tight butt in the shower raced into her mind. She'd have to get those kinds of thoughts under control and the sooner the better. It had been way too long since she'd had good sex and with those thoughts popping up she'd have a hard time getting through the morning without jumping Cody's bones. And that in itself, was not a bad idea.

Sex with Cody would have to be satisfying. To her, he just looked like he could handle whatever she wanted from him. Right now, she'd like him to just turn around, pick her up so she could wrap her legs around his waist, shove her up against the wall and make her scream with pleasure.

"Anything you need?" asked Cody as he opened the passenger side door of his truck and stood back so Harley could get in.

The question caught her off guard for a moment. Simultaneously, she thought hot sex and opened her mouth, but caught herself before she spewed it out.

"No, no," she stuttered, "I'm fine."

"Great, then we'll head on out," said Cody as he handed her the seatbelt before closing the truck's door. Walking around behind the truck, he crawled into the driver's seat.

"So where are we going?" asked Harley.

"Back yonder a little way," said Cody as he nodded in the direction he headed after cranking the truck and putting it in gear.

"Behind the house?' asked Harley.

"Yep, not far. Just figured it'd be easier to drive as close as we can get before we have to start walking."

"Well, this sounds interesting. And just how far do we walk once we get there?" Harley asked.

"Oh, it's only a hop, skip and a jump away. Hold on now, this might get a little bit bumpy," Cody said as he steered the truck over the cattle grate and into the open field.

"Did Aunt Tilly have cattle here?" asked Harley.

"No, but several of the farmers around here have a few cows and they use Tilly's land for grazing at different times."

"Well, that's interesting. Did she rent it out or what?"

"Naw, if you needed some space you just let her know and you were welcome to use her land."

"She sounds like she was a really nice person."

"She was. You really didn't know her at all, did you?"

"Nope. Probably wouldn't have known anything about her at all if it weren't for the cards and presents she sent."

Sit right there a minute and let me run around to your door and we'll go watch a few flowers grow."

"Okay," replied Harley as she straightened back up in the truck seat.

Cody opened his door, ran around behind the truck and opened Harley's.

"Come on," he said, "it's not far."

Harley slid down out of the truck and took hold of Cody's arm and walked along beside him down a small pathway until they came out in a clearing that sat on top of a hill.

In front of her lay a tiny valley with a small stream rambling across it. The entire valley had exploded in color. Flowers of all colors, shapes and sizes grew in every direction.

Harley gasped at the sight.

"Oh my gosh, how the ..."

"Aunt Tilly painted it."

"What do you mean, she painted it?"

"Well, sometimes she'd walk out here and wander around. She always brought flower seeds with her and she'd toss 'em around as she walked. After a few years the place was nothing but color. Most of the folks around here know it exists but a lot of 'em have never seen it though. And, nobody tells outsiders about it."

"But I'm an outsider," said Harley.

"No, I don't think you are. I think you belong here. I think it feels like home to you."

"I wouldn't know. I don't know what home feels like."

"It feels like this," he said as he took her in his arms. Slowly he lifted her chin and looked deep into her eyes before bringing his lips down to gently touch hers. Her lips felt warm and soft and he wanted more of her. He needed more of her. This woman had worked her way under his skin without even trying.

From that first glimpse of her standing beside her bike and taking off her helmet and all that long curly hair falling down her back, he was a gonner. Now all he had to do was convince her.

He deepened the kiss, his tongue demanding entrance to her warm, moist mouth. She tasted like honey.

She responded to his demand. She wanted this man. He did things to her without even knowing it.

Her arms encircled his neck and her fingers found their way into his hair. Her breathing was quick and shallow. Her heart pounding a rhythm in her ears and all she could think was more.

She needed more. Wanted more. Could this be love? The thought stopped her cold. Quickly she withdrew from him.

Cody felt the moment she stiffened. He knew something had stopped her from letting herself go. Something deep down she was afraid to let go of. He would give her time. He would keep searching for the key that opened the rest of her to her own desires.

"I, I—" stammered Harley.

"It's okay. We have time. Lots of time. Come on let's go watch some flowers grow and some bees pollinate."

Cody led her down among the flowers and sat down on the ground. He motioned for her to sit down beside him.

"Now, no talking. Just listening. Listen to the sounds all around."

Cody lay back, folding his hands behind his head and closing his eyes, he listened.

Harley sat still for a few minutes, looking and listening. The flowers were vibrant and beautiful. She watched a honey bee land on a nearby flower and watched as it sucked the nectar from it. It's little legs bulging with its find.

This certainly beat the hustle and bustle of the cities she'd been in. Places where nobody knew her name or anything about her. Places where nobody cared anything about her. Places where nobody cared if she lived or died.

Here, she had learned about some of the people and they had learned things about her.

She wondered what it would have been like to live here in this place with someone who cared about her. Someone like Aunt Tilly who cared about other people's children. Maybe with someone like that, they would care for a child whose own mother didn't want them.

What could she have done that was bad enough to be left behind? She needed that answer. An answer she would never have because she couldn't even remember what her mother looked like. As far as she knew, she could be standing beside her on a street corner and never know it. That answer would never come.

Harley watched a butterfly land on a flower next to her. It was peaceful here in this valley. She could hear the rippling of the water flowing lazily downstream. A slight breeze played with wisps of her hair. It seemed almost therapeutic.

"Penny for your thoughts," said Cody, as he lay staring up at Harley.

She turned her head sideways and looked down at him before deciding to lay down on her stomach, prop herself up on her elbows and look at him.

"I could get used to watching the flowers grow," said Harley. "I mean, it seems like time just doesn't exist here. I know it does, and all, but—"

"Oh there's no need to convince me. I love this place. Sitting right here in this meadow during the spring time, watching the world wake after a winter nap, it's something you don't get a chance to see elsewhere. And in the summer, well, there's just nothing like it. And, watching the squirrels gather nuts and stuff in the fall for the upcoming winter hibernation, well, like I said, there's just nothing like it."

"I can only imagine what that'd be like."

"You know, you've got a house here now. You could stay. You could walk out here during any season of the year and slow down, watch the flowers grow."

"I've never been in one place long enough to get attached to it."

"Well, if you keep the house, you would always have a place to come home to."

"I would, wouldn't I? I wouldn't have to stay here all the time. I could get on my bike and ride out any time I felt like things were closing in on me, but, I'd always be able to come back home."

CHAPTER SEVENTEEN

Morning came early for Harley. Thoughts of Cody invaded her mind. She'd enjoyed spending time with him and smelling the flowers yesterday. She'd heard him come in this morning and the shower water come on. Thoughts of him standing underneath the stream of hot water naked had her day-dreaming of being in the shower with him. Tingles ran down her skin and collected in her lower region making her breathing shallow and her heart rate quicken.

She needed to get Aunt Tilly's house taken care of and move on. Getting involved with a man at this point in her life was not something she cared to do. This one could have her wrapped in knots if she wasn't careful.

But, she'd had her fill of men. The last one, she hadn't even had sex with and he was nothing but trouble on all levels. She was glad she'd gotten away from him after his last drunken episode. Being on the back of a motorcycle when the driver was blitzed out of his gourd was not good.

But then, she did like this little sleepy town. It felt like home, or at least home the way she envisioned it would feel. Growing up without a mom had been difficult. Understanding why her mom left her was not something she understood at all.

Her dad did his best in raising her but being a military man, he'd had to bring in housekeepers or ship her off to stay with some other military family whenever he was shipped some place she couldn't go. Those were the hard times. She never belonged, and it was that feeling of belonging she wanted to feel encase her like a cocoon. There would be warmth, love, hugs, closeness – all those things she'd never had before. There just wasn't any room for a man in her picturesque life.

Rolling over in her bed, she pulled the covers up closer around her neck. Glancing over at the clock on the night stand, she groaned. She needed a shower and a cup of hot coffee to help get her morning started.

Shoving the covers back, she sat up on the side of the bed, and stretched her legs out in front of her, flexing her toes and feeling the pull on her calves.

She heard Cody's truck pulling into the barn and moments later she could hear water running. Imagining that hot body of his standing in the shower with water running down his chest sent tingles down her spine.

She needed coffee but not having a kitchen in her part of the house meant she'd have to get dressed and head to Katy's Kitchen to get a cup. So she'd have to shower first then get dressed and head over to Katy's for coffee and breakfast. Maybe she'd see about picking up a coffee pot today but that didn't take care of her immediate need.

Heading into the bathroom, she stripped out of the t-shirt and panties she'd slept in and turned on the shower adjusting it to just the right temperature before climbing in.

* * *

Cody stood in the kitchen placing fresh coffee grounds into the coffeemaker and filling it with water before turning it on. Wanting a quick bite of breakfast before crawling into bed, he opened the fridge and pulled out a package of frozen sausage links along with a couple of eggs to fry.

Hearing the shower come on upstairs, he grinned, hoping he would hear another blood curdling scream. He could get used to saving spiders.

Placing the sausage in the microwave, he turned it on and turned to grab a coffee cup and plate from the cabinet. Suddenly, he heard a noise coming from the direction of his bedroom. Unsure of exactly what it was, he laid the eggs on the counter and headed in that direction.

Entering the bedroom, he caught sight of a small stream of brown water falling from the ceiling and landing squarely in the middle of his bed.

"Damn!" he cursed, as he turned and ran towards the hallway and the stairs to Harley's apartment.

Reaching for the doorknob, he turned it but found it wouldn't open.

"Damnation!" he cursed as he began banging on the door. "Harley, Harley, turn off the water! Turn off the water!"

No answer.

Cody banged his fist against the door as hard as he could as he continued yelling.

"Harley, turn off the damn water! Turn off the water!"

A minute later, he heard the shower stop and ran back to his bedroom. The dirty water was still leaking from the ceiling and soaking his bed.

Running into the kitchen, Cody grabbed the mop bucket he kept underneath the kitchen sink and hurried back into his bedroom and placed it on the bed to catch the water.

Hurrying back to the hallway he raised his fist to bang on the door just as Harley opened it.

"You banging on my door?" she asked.

"You could say that. Your shower leaks."

"What?"

"Your shower, it's leaking all over my bed."

"What?"

"There's water coming from the ceiling and it's pouring onto my bed. Your bathroom is right above my bedroom. Pipes are leaking."

"Let me see," said Harley as she headed toward Cody's bedroom.

Cody's gaze fell to Harley's backside as she swished and swayed her way to his bedroom. He liked the fact she was wrapped in a towel with her wet hair clinging to her shoulders. Damn but she was nice to look at.

"Oh gross!" said Harley as she caught sight of the brown wet spot on Cody's bed and the bucket of nasty water that water was still dripping into from the ceiling. "That's nasty. You sure it's from the shower. I mean, it's brown and all."

"Pipes are probably rusty and just finally rusted into. It may just be the drain pipe. You won't be able to use it until you get a plumber over here and get it fixed."

"A plumber. Geez, how much is that going to cost me?"

"I'm guessing a few hundred bucks at least."

"Well, I don't have a few hundred bucks at the moment."

"Guess you won't be taking another shower anytime soon then," said Cody as he leaned against the bathroom door jam."

"But I've got shampoo in my hair. I need to rinse it out."

"Looks to me like you've got a problem."

Harley stood there looking from the soggy bed to the drippy ceiling and back to Cody.

"I don't suppose you'd let me borrow your shower until I get the insurance money from my dad's policy. Once I get that, I can fix the place up a bit. But, until then, I'm broke."

"Tell you what. I think it'd be safer if you just didn't use your bathroom at all. For anything, if you get my drift. There's no telling what shape any of those ol' pipes are in and I'd sure hate to be sleeping when your toilet decides to start leaking. You can come down and use mine when you need. In the meantime, I'll turn the water off to the upstairs to keep anything else from leaking."

"Thank you, I really appreciate it. I'll try not to bother you too much."

"It's a deal then. Go ahead and finish your shower and I'll get this mattress stripped and take it outside so it can dry out. And, when you're finished, there's coffee on the counter. Help yourself."

"Bless you. I'll pick up a coffee pot today, but I was trying to get showered and dressed so I could head over to Katy's for some coffee and breakfast."

"Listen, if you're going to be here fixing this place up until my lease runs out, how about if we work out a deal. We can be roommates, you can use the kitchen, the shower, there's plenty of food in there and that kind of stuff and you can take it off my rent. That'll help us both."

"Oh that's a wonderful idea! Thank you."

"We can work out the details later, but for now, use my bathroom to finish your shower and I'll head down to the basement and turn off the water to the upstairs."

"Great! I won't be long. I'll just go rinse the soap off, run back upstairs, get dressed and then come back down and grab a cup of coffee. I'll be quiet as a mouse. I'll do my best not to disturb your sleep," she said as she turned to head back upstairs.

You already disturb my sleep.

Cody watched her backside sway as she walked away.

CHAPTER EIGHTEEN

Twenty minutes later Harley quietly tiptoed down the stairs and headed into the kitchen. Her senses were assaulted with wonderful smelling food aromas. Cody was cooking something and it smelled delicious. Her stomach rumbled with approval.

"I don't know what you're cooking, but it smells delicious," said Harley as she walked into the kitchen and poured herself a cup of coffee.

"Well, you're just in time. I've been slaving over a hot stove for hours to fix my delicacy of microwave sausage links and scrambled eggs. Hope you're hungry," Cody smiled as he dished up the eggs onto plates and placed a couple of sausage links on each before motioning with his hand, holding one plate, for her to take a seat at the kitchen breakfast counter.

"Can I pour you a cup of coffee?"

"Sure," he said, "just refresh what's in my cup."

"Okay," she said as she refilled his cup and took it with her to the counter.

"Dig in," said Cody as he took his cup from her hand. Taking a sip, he sat the cup down as he picked up his own silverware.

"It really does look good," she said as she cut into the sausage and took a bite. "Ummmmmmm! This is just delicious."

"Not much to it. Just pop it into the microwave."

"Well, it does have a great taste. Microwave stuff usually isn't this good."

"I like this particular brand. It's good."

"Well, thank you for fixing it. How about if I cook tomorrow morning?"

"I could get used to that," said Cody.

"Well, I didn't say I was any good at it," said Harley as she laughed.

Cody liked the sound of her laughter. It was as heartfelt as a child's and he loved the sparkle that showed in her eyes as she laughed.

"My mama always taught me to eat whatever was put before me and not to complain about it, too," Cody replied.

"She obviously never tasted my cooking either. You can judge for yourself tomorrow."

"So, here's my plan for the day. I thought I'd get a few hours' sleep this morning, then I can start work on those stairs outside. May take me a couple days to get them in working order. Once you get your money you can decide what you want me to fix and in what order, but I'd suggest maybe starting with the plumbing."

"Yeah, I'm kinda thinking along that line myself. Running downstairs in the middle of the night is not going to be fun, I don't think," she said as she laughed.

"Depends on what you're running downstairs for." Cody grinned.

"Is having sex all you ever think about?"

"Nope. Sometimes I think about not having it but that thought doesn't last long."

"I'll just bet not."

Cody took the last sip of his coffee.

"I hate to eat and run, but I need to get some sleep. Take your time. Finish your breakfast and I'll see you later on," said Cody as he stood and grabbed his dishes.

"Just drop those dishes in the sink. I'll take care of them as soon as I'm finished here."

"Thanks," said Cody as he placed his dishes in the sink.

Grabbing his gun belt from the hook on the wall beside the breakfast counter and headed down the hall towards his bedroom.

Sleep was definitely not going to be easy. There was just something about this woman that had gotten under his skin the moment he first laid eyes on her. She intrigued the hell out of him when she rode into town and something about her still intrigued the hell out of him.

He just needed to keep his focus and keep his heart secured tightly under wraps. It wouldn't be easy.

Harley sat in silence as she listened to Cody's footsteps fade away into the sound of his bedroom door clicking shut. The word 'family' floated through her mind. Must be the house. Family had owned this old house and it seemed to take her in and wrap her in its loving arms.

She didn't remember ever having visited here as a child, so it must just be the ghost of

85

Aunt Tilly reminding her that this house held family.

Thoughts of her mother floated into her brain before she could stop them. She'd carried the baggage with her since the day her mother left. What had she done to make her mother not love her? What had she done to make her mother leave and never come back? How could her mother have just walked out and not taken her, too? Tears rimmed her eyes before she caught herself and shoved those thoughts back to the cavernous hole in her heart and shut the door again.

CHAPTER NINETEEN

Flo's was abuzz this morning with the latest gossip. It'd taken all of two minutes after Flo opened the boutique's door for Agnes to arrive with the morning's hot topic.

"Did you hear?" asked Agnes as she set her purse on the station's counter and took a seat in the chair.

"Must not have. What've you heard already this morning?" asked Flo.

"The Reverend. Haven't you heard about the Reverend's little problem. I swear, I don't know what this world is coming to when the Reverend's out doing who knows what with who knows who!"

"Well, girl, go on and spill it. You've got me curious now. What's the good Reverend done now?"

"I'd watch who you're calling 'good,'" replied Agnes, "I mean after all, he wasn't so good while he was getting' what he's got. Well maybe he was good, but he shouldn't have been good with whoever he was good with."

"Agnes!" exclaimed Flo, "What the hell are you talkin' about, girl!"

"Oh, I'm sorry. It's just that the good Reverend has got hisself a case of the syphilis."

"What? What do you mean?"

"Just what I said. Reverend Lollar has a case of syphilis and today's him and the missus' thirtieth anniversary, too."

"You talking about our Reverend Lollar?"

"Yep, the same. See, he was over in Tuscaloosa getting his physical the other day, you know, and they always do these different blood tests. Well, it seems his came back that he had the syphilis."

"Now how'd you find that out?" asked Flo as she combed out Agnes silver blue short curly hair.

"You know, Mavis' daughter's girl. Well, she has a friend who works over at the lab in Tuscaloosa and her friend saw the results and well, you know, you can't keep a juicy bit of news like that to yourself. Anyway, she mentioned it to Mavis' daughter who told her mama right away."

"Well I'll be. As far as I know, you can only get syphilis one way and that's sex. And I'll just bet he's already given it to that poor sweet wife of his. I mean, that poor thing," said Flo.

"I know. He's out tomcatting around and brings it home and gives it to her. I mean, that's just like a man. And him a man of the cloth to boot. Can't keep it zipped up in his pants for nothing," Agnes continued.

"Well, I just don't know what to think. Does she know yet?" asked Flo as she took the scissors and clipped at Agnes' hair.

"Lawd, have mercy!" said Agnes. "I never thought of that."

CHAPTER TWENTY

Harley took a look at the boxes stacked all over the place. Deciding she needed to go through them and decide what she could throw away and what she wanted to keep, she punched through the yellowed masking tape that was trying to hold the closest box lid closed.

Pulling out the first item, she unfolded an old apron that, while it was clean, was stained from many years of use in the kitchen. Digging down further through the box, she found nothing but various clothes obviously belonging to her Aunt Tilly. She marked the box as clothes to donate. But the thought struck her that she really could use a little money and she might be able to have a yard sale and maybe make a few dollars to get her by until the insurance check came in.

After stacking the first ten boxes full of clothes next to the door, she opened another one. It was a large one standing in the corner.

Oh my gosh, Christmas. She stood staring at the green tree branches. Childhood memories flooded her mind. Christmas had never come to her house. She knew it was because she was bad. So bad even her own mother had left her. There weren't any birthday parties. There was no Christmas tree or Christmas decorations. No celebration.

She had seen her friends' homes decorated for the Christmas season. There was always a tree laden with decorations surrounded by brightly wrapped packages. After hearing their tales of family celebrations, gifts, traditions and everything that went with Christmas, she had spent many December nights crying herself to sleep. She had been so bad that not only did her mother leave, but she was so bad even Christmas never came to her house. A tear dripped off her cheek and onto the floor.

She began furiously opening other boxes until she'd found all the Christmas ones. She retrieved the tree stand from the box she found it in and stood the tree in it. Minutes later, branches spread out, she began placing the strings of Christmas lights on it starting at the top and working her way down, swiping the tears from her eyes as she worked. Taking ornaments from their boxes, she examined each one in detail before placing it on the tree. The twinkling star tree topper was the last to take its place on top of the tree.

Harley stood back and gazed at the decorated tree. Her first one as far back as she could remember.

She sat down on the floor in front of the decorated tree and began looking through old photo albums she'd found packed in another box. She carefully took them out one by one, looking through each before giving it a place underneath the tree.

Harley didn't know most of the people in the albums, but she did recognize the one of her mom holding her as a baby and her dad standing beside them. They looked happy.

It was the same photo her dad had kept on the nightstand in his bedroom. There were others of her until the age of three and that's where they stopped. It was as though she ceased to exist after that time. That's how she felt, too. She had simply stopped existing when her mother left.

There were photos of her mother with another lady she assumed was Aunt Tilly. She'd take one of the photos to Katy next time she went. Katy would be able to tell her if the other lady in the photo was indeed Aunt Tilly.

The last album placed, she sat watching the tree lights twinkle. She longed for all she had missed. Hours passed as she sat with tears trickling down her face. All she could think was why? Why was I so bad? What did I do? What did I do that made my mother run away? What is it about me that made her not love me? If I'm so bad my own mother couldn't love me, no one will ever be able to love me.

CHAPTER TWENTY-ONE

Cody had knocked on the doorway but when he didn't get an answer, he assumed Harley was out. Wanting to check the damage in her bathroom to see how extensive the water line repair would need to be, he opened the door and walked up the stairs. Seeing Harley sitting on the floor in front of a fully decorated Christmas tree, he stopped.

Even though it was July in Shady Rivers and hot as blazes, she had started a fire in the fireplace and, at the same time, had the air conditioner on full blast.

Not wanting to intrude on her private moments, he was about to turn and head back down the stairs, but at that moment, Harley turned her face toward him and he saw.

He saw such raw pain in her eyes. Tears streaked her swollen face. It looked as though she'd been crying for hours. Her pain stabbed at his heart and he walked over and sat down beside her. He pulled her body into his arms, rested her head on his shoulder and began to rock. Words weren't needed.

Harley only took a second before she fell into his embrace, dissolving into tears. Her shoulders heaved while her breath came in hard sobs as she cried out her pent-up three-year old's terror at being left alone without her mommy.

Cody smoothed away strands of hair from her wet cheeks, still cradling her in his arms.

"Hold on tight, darlin', he whispered as his lips brushed against her forehead. "I'm right here. I'm not going anywhere."

Harley clutched his shirt in her balled-up fists while her tears soaked into his shirt as she cried out her torment.

Finally, her sobs quieted. Occasionally a lone hiccup escaped as testimony to the emotional storm which had passed through.

Cody wasn't sure how much time had passed before Harley spoke.

"I'm sorry," said Harley, as she tried to pull away from his embrace.

"Don't be," he said still holding her close. "Wanna talk about it?"

"It's nothing really," she said as she pulled away. "I ran across all this Christmas stuff. I just never had a Christmas is all."

"What do you mean you never had a Christmas?"

Memories of the Christmases he'd spent with his mom and Angel flashed through his mind. He missed those times.

"My dad wasn't into celebrating holidays and stuff like that, so we never had Christmas."

"That must have been hard on you and your mom."

"Mom, as you call her, left when I was three. Dad was in the military."

94

"Wait, wait a minute. Your mother left when you were three?"

Harley sat there a minute. Why had she told him that? She'd never told anyone about her private hell before. But it'd been easy with Cody. He seemed to open the lid she kept on those things without even trying. She just opened her mouth and it slid out.

"Yeah, it was no big deal," said Harley as she turned her face away so he wouldn't see the pain she knew registered there.

"Well, I consider it a big deal. Do you know where she is now?"

"Not really. She had always wanted to live in France, sit in the outside coffee shops and write so I guess that's where she went."

"And she just left you here with your dad."

"Yeah, guess I didn't fit in as a character in her idyllic life."

"Well, darlin', looking at that life from an outsider's perspective, it certainly don't register as idyllic to me. I'll bet you there hasn't been a day gone by she hasn't thought about you."

Harley laughed. "Yeah, like she gives a rat's ass about me. You don't just up and dump your three-year-old kid and hightail it out of the country without some damn good reason. That reason was me. I was so bad, she didn't want me. She wanted to live on the French Riviera, write and flirt with Frenchmen and Dad and I neither one fit into that picture. So, she just up and left one day and never came back. I waited, yes, I waited. I was three years old for God's sake!" Harley felt the tears stinging the corners of her eyes again. This melt down was not supposed to be happening.

CHAPTER TWENTY-TWO

Cody opened up his arms.

"Come here."

Harley fell into his embrace. She needed to feel wanted. She needed to feel loved.

"You've never cried for your mom before, have you?"

The no-response he got told him what he needed to know. Pulling her tighter, he drew her body up against him until he felt she had become a part of him. The thought of precious cargo floated through his mind. He was definitely in trouble now.

"I grew up spending more time living with other people than I did with my dad. I had housekeepers when he was state-side and lived with other military families when he wasn't. So, I just never had any connection with real family. I knew my mother existed somewhere and that Aunt Tilly existed somewhere, too, and that was it."

"Didn't you ever wonder about Tilly?"

"Oh sure, I did. All the time. I asked my dad once if I could go live with her instead of somebody else's family. Had to clean our entire bathroom with a toothbrush for that thought so I never brought it up again."

"What on earth for? Why did he object to you living with family?"

"He just objected to anybody who was connected with my mother."

"Well, not that it does you any good now, but you would have loved Aunt Tilly. She was as sweet as she could be. Was always seeing to it that all the kids around here were taken care of and that we all had plenty of cookies." Cody laughed. "I swear, I think there were kids from other towns who came by Aunt Tilly's just to get some of her cookies."

"She sounds like she really loved kids."

"Oh, she did. Took in a lot of us strays."

"You lived with her?" asked Harley as she pulled away and sat up to look him in the face.

"No, no, not exactly. My father was never in the picture, so my mom worked two jobs taking care of me and my sister which meant that my sister and I were on our own most of the time. Now don't go holding that against my mom 'cause she did the best she could."

"At least she didn't leave you."

"No, but, still, it was hard on her and on my sister and I, too. But Aunt Tilly took us on as her official duty. She made sure we had what we needed, and she made sure we towed the line, too. She watched over my sister and I like a hawk. Couldn't get away with anything."

"I think I would have liked her, too," said Harley as she took the bottom edge of her shirt and wiped at her eyes. "Listen, I'm really sorry to have involved you in my meltdown."

"Don't be sorry. I'm glad I could be here for you. Listen, I have an idea. I have some hot chocolate mix downstairs. How about if I go make us a cup and bring it back up here and we can sit here and have Christmas together."

"You'd do that for me. You'd sit here with me and pretend it's Christmas?"

"Sure. I just happen to like Christmas. You know any Christmas songs?" he asked as he stood and pulled her up with him.

"*Jingle Bells* and maybe *Frosty the Snowman*," she replied as a smile spread across her face.

"Okay, *Jingle Bells* and *Frosty* it is. Now, you go wash all those tears off your face and I'll get the chocolate," he said as he kissed her forehead, turned and started out the door singing a loud version of Jingle Bells as he went.

Excitement coursed through Harley's veins and something else she couldn't quite put words to coursed through the rest of her body as she watched him walk out the door.

Moments later Cody returned with two cups of hot chocolate in hand as Harley came out of the bathroom.

"Here you are," said Cody as he handed her a cup. "Now, it's Christmas Eve so we'll need a blanket to wrap up in while we sip our chocolate."

"I've got one," she said handing him back her cup. "Hold this while I get it."

Cody took the cup and waited until she returned from the bedroom with a blanket in hand.

"Can you grab the cushions off the sofa there and toss them on the floor in front of the tree."

"Yep," said Harley. She couldn't believe Cody was actually doing Christmas with her and he seemed to be having fun, too. Grabbing the sofa cushions, she put them on the floor.

"Sit down and then I'll hand you the chocolate," said Cody.

Harley took a seat and reached up taking the cup of hot chocolate from his hand.

Cody sat down beside her.

"My mom always had us open gifts to each other on Christmas Eve and Santa always brought my sister and I a present on Christmas morning."

"I'll bet that was fun. What'd you get?" asked Harley as she sipped her chocolate.

"Different things. One year I got a BB gun and my sister got a doll she'd been wanting. There was always an apple, an orange and some nuts in our Christmas stockings. And, usually, a piece or two of candy," said Cody as he slipped off his shoes and stretched out his legs. "Take off your shoes. You can't sit in front of a Christmas tree with your shoes on."

Harley laughed as she removed her shoes and tossed them aside.

"It's also customary to remove the rest of your clothes, too," Cody said as he grinned at her.

"What? I don't think that was ever part of your Christmas," she said as she laughed.

"You can't blame a guy for trying."

"Well, good try, but it ain't gonna happen, Barney Fife."

"Here," said Cody as he reached into his jeans' pocket and took out a small package wrapped in Christmas paper.

"Oh my gosh, what's this?" said Harley, surprise registering in her voice.

"Like I said, you're supposed to get a present on Christmas Eve." He smiled at her as she took the present from his hand.

"But—"

"No buts. It's just something I grabbed while I was downstairs that I thought you might like. After all, you can't have Christmas without getting a present you've always wanted."

"So, you had something downstairs that I've always been wanting?" she asked laughing.

"Yep, sure did. Been waiting a long time for you to come get it, too!" He laughed.

"Yeah, I'll bet you have."

"Go ahead and open it."

Cody watched as Harley tore into the little package, tossing Christmas paper onto the floor. She looked like a kid opening a gift on Christmas morning. Excitement shown in her eyes. Something moved off kilter inside his heart at that moment.

CHAPTER TWENTY-THREE

Harley stared at the snow globe in her hand. There was a house with a large window so you could see in. There was a mom, a dad, a boy, a girl and a dog. It was Christmas. The tree was up and packages were strewn underneath. It was the family she'd wished for but never had.

Tears rimmed her eyes as she looked over at Cody. Her hands trembled, her breath caught. There was no other gift that could have made her any happier than her little make belief family.

"I—"

"No need. Let me tell you about that little globe."

"It has a story?" she asked as she wiped at her eyes.

"It definitely has a story. It used to sit in the window over at Dottie's Five and Dime. I liked walking by and looking in the window. They always had things us kids wanted. Well, I wanted that snow globe. Didn't tell anybody. I mean, after all, I was a boy and boys didn't want things like snow globes. But to me, that snow globe had what I wanted."

"What did you want?" asked Harley.

"That," he said as he pointed to the scene inside it. "I wanted that family. I had the mom and the sister and even the dog, but we were missing the dad. Don't know how she knew, but it was Christmas Eve day and my mom was working. My sister and I were at Aunt Tilly's having cookies and waiting for mom to get off work. Aunt Tilly got up from the kitchen table. She said she had something she needed to give us, so she went to the other room and came back with a small package for me and one for my sister."

"Christmas presents."

"Yep. My sister opened hers first. It was a little gold locket. Inside was a dime and a picture of me."

"What was the dime for?"

"Aunt Tilly said anytime Angel found herself needing help, she should use that dime to call her big brother and if she couldn't get me, then she should call Aunt Tilly. Phone calls were a dime back then."

"What a thoughtful gift."

"Yes, it was."

"And what was in your package?"

"Just what I wanted. That little snow globe. I never did figure out how she knew. But she gave it to me and said that someday my wish would come true."

"I can't take this. This is yours. It means something to you," said Harley as she offered the snow globe to him.

"Keep it. It means something to you, too. And it'll mean more to me to know that your first Christmas present was a family from Aunt Tilly, too."

"I don't know what to say," said Harley.

"Just say you'll keep it and make us both happy," said Cody as he grinned at her.

"Yes, thank you," said Harley as she threw her arms around his neck and gave him a hug. A sensation of something she couldn't quite name flowed through her veins. It was a good feeling. Realizing what she was doing, she began to pull back.

Cody's gaze caught hers and she was lost in frosty blue eyes. It seemed as though he knew her deepest thoughts. He was sweet and sensitive. Her heart skipped a beat as she realized she wanted this man. There was just something about him. Something that felt like coming home.

Cody lost himself in hauntingly beautiful hazel eyes. What was it about this woman that made him want to lose himself in the depths of her soul? His gaze fell to her lips. Soft, kissable lips. He wanted to taste the sweetness of her and lose himself in her charms. His lips found hers hesitant at first, but passion ignited the flames and he deepened the kiss as she opened her lips to him allowing tongues to dance a dance as old as time itself. His hands clung to the softness of her hair as he cupped the sides of her head wanting to keep her lips tasting his.

Harley lost herself in his kiss. He ignited a passion in her she didn't even know existed until that moment. All her mind could think was more. I need more. But, her mind played tricks on her as it began to relieve her insecurities. Thoughts of he'll leave you, too, surfaced and she felt herself grow tense. She realized Cody must have felt it, too, as he broke the kiss at that moment.

105

"You okay?" he asked.

"I, I—"

"It's okay. I shouldn't have let that happen, but I've been wanting to do that, and I just couldn't help myself."

"If I were to tell you the truth, I kinda wanted it, too."

Cody smiled down at her.

"Tell you what. Now that we've got that out of our system, how about if we just sit here, enjoy our chocolate and enjoy our first Christmas together."

"I like that idea," she said as she laughed and snuggled back into his arms.

Cody began humming *Jingle Bells*.

CHAPTER TWENTY-FOUR

Harley couldn't remember ever having such a fun day as she'd had yesterday with Cody. They'd drank hot chocolate in front of a fire in the middle of a hot, humid July, sang Christmas songs so loud she was sure if there'd been neighbors close by, they would have heard them.

Cody had seemed to go out of his way to make sure she had enjoyed her Christmas. After that one little kiss, he'd been a perfect gentleman the rest of the time. She had really had a good time and she wanted more days like that. More simple, fun times with—

The word family darted into her mind. Was that really how it felt to have family. It was a good feeling and she wanted more of it.

Pushing that thought out of her mind, she crawled out of bed and headed downstairs for a shower.

She quietly opened the door into Cody's part of the house and quickly headed toward the hall bath. Passing the living room, she caught sight of Cody asleep on the couch with a woman snuggled with her backside toward him. They were both sleeping.

Her heart stopped as what she was seeing registered in her brain. Cody had a girlfriend. And, apparently, she'd slept over last night. What a fool she'd been! That kiss. She even let herself think she might be good enough to enjoy a family. Well, just like her mom, Cody showed her she wasn't worth anything. He'd just been entertaining himself until he could be with someone who was worthy of his efforts. Well, she'd not make that mistake again.

She finished her shower, got dressed and headed to Katy's.

* * *

Hearing the familiar jingle as the cafe's door opened, Katy looked up from taking Agnes Moorhead and Sarah Tuckerman's breakfast order to see Harley step inside.

"Hey girl," yelled Katy. "Take a seat and I'll be with you in a jiff."

Harley nodded and walked to the counter and took a seat, thoughts of Cody occupying her mind.

"Well, well, well," said a familiar voice from behind her.

Harley cringed at the sound, her breathing quickened and for a moment she wanted to run, but she realized there was safety here inside.

"What are you doing here?" she asked.

"I told you I'd find you," he said.

Harley flinched at the pain she felt as he grabbed hold of her upper arm and forcibly pulled her from the stool.

"Let go of me," she yelled as he continued dragging her toward the door.

Katy looked up at the commotion. She saw Gus through the order window as he was hurrying out the kitchen door and headed toward Harley, meat cleaver in his hand.

At that moment, the restaurant door opened and Spence walked in for his morning coffee.

"Well, well, what have we here?" asked Spence as he quickly assessed the situation. "Miss Harley, is this fellow bothering you?"

The man quickly shielded himself as he drug Harley in front of him.

"I don't have no beef with you. This here's my woman and she's coming with me. Now if you'll step aside—"

"If I were you, before I made another move and got myself in a whole lot of trouble, I'd take a look around," said Spence as a wicked smile crossed his lips.

The man stood perfectly still for a moment, then glanced to his side. He saw two older ladies at a table with handguns pointed directly at him. He glanced back toward Spence.

Spence nodded in the other direction.

Again, the man glanced to that side and saw four older looking men with even larger handguns pointed directly at him and at the edge of the counter stood the cook with a meat cleaver in hand.

Assessing the situation, the man said, "I just want to talk to my woman here."

"I am not your woman! Now take your hands off me!" growled Harley as she twisted out of his grip. "I have a no contact order against this man."

"Well, now, the way I see this is you're going to do one of two things. You can either come with me peaceably or with all these guns pointed at you, I can call the undertaker."

The man put his hands in the air.

Spence walked over and placed his handcuffs on the man before leading him to the doorway.

"Harley, I'll need you to stop by the office when you've finished your breakfast, if you don't mind," Spence called over his shoulder as he opened the door.

"Sure, Sheriff," replied Harley as she and Katy stood clutching each other.

"Girl, what the hell was that all about?" asked Katy.

"Long story."

"Well, you come on over here and sit down. I'll get you a fresh cup of coffee. Actually, I'll make you my specialty. I call it a Shady Sunrise. It'll help you relax a little and I think you need it," said Katy as she scurried behind the counter.

"You okay?" asked Gus as he came over and draped his arm around Harley's shoulders.

"Yeah, I'm fine," said Harley as she let out a big sigh. "And thank you, Gus. I appreciate you being there for me. Actually," said Harley as she turned around on her stool, "thanks to all of you for having my back. It's much appreciated."

"No problem," said Agnes.

"Yeah, not a problem at all," replied the others all at once.

Turning back around to Katy, Harley whispered, "Does everyone around here carry guns?"

Katy laughed, "Lordy, hon, we all grew up with guns. Most of us could shoot before we could walk. It's just a way of life down here. I mean, you can't go walking in the cow pasture or down by the creek or any place for that matter without something to take care of the vermin around here. I mean there are snakes down here that if you get bit, you may as well just sit down and smoke a cigarette because you gonna die before you're done smoking and they ain't nothing nobody can do about it."

"Geez. Thanks for warning me."

"If you ain't got a gun, honey, you need to get yourself one and learn how to use it. You just be careful out there on Tilly's place and watch where you're stepping when you go outside. Here you are, one Shady Sunrise," said Katy as she sat the frothy coffee drink in front of Harley.

"This looks good and smells heavenly," said Harley as she picked up the cup and took a sip. "Oh my gosh, this is so-o-o-o tasty. Don't think I've ever had anything quite this delicious. What in the world is in it?"

"Well, there's hot coffee, of course, but the rest, now that's my little secret," said Katy as she smiled.

"You need to sell that secret to one of those coffee houses. You'd be rich!"

"Naw, money can't buy what I have here in Shady Rivers. Money just usually brings you a ton more trouble. I got everything I need right here. A place to live, some food to eat and good family and friends who'd give me the shirt off their backs if they thought I needed it. Now that's something money can't buy."

"I reckon it is," replied Harley.

111

Gus, placing an order in the order window, smiled at Katy's words. Yes, he would give Katy the shirt off his back or anything else for that matter, if she needed it. She was a rose among thorns.

CHAPTER TWENTY-FIVE

"How 'bout if I get you some breakfast now?" asked Katy.

"Thanks, Katy, but I seem to have lost my appetite at the moment. I'll stop back in as soon as it returns," Harley said as she smiled and headed toward the door.

Taking her time, Harley walked over to the Sheriff's office. Cody wouldn't be there which was just fine with her. He would be sleeping since he would be working the evening shift.

Opening the door to the Sheriff's office, Harley stepped inside. Her nerves seemed to be on edge with the thought of Todd Dillard being locked up somewhere inside the jail.

"Come on in," said Spence as he stood up behind his desk. "Just doing a little paperwork here. Have a seat, have a seat," he said as he motioned toward the chair sitting in front of his desk.

"Thanks, Sheriff," replied Harley as she walked over and sat down. Her gaze flitted around the office.

"Don't worry," said Spence picking up on her unease. "He's tucked away back there behind some good steel bars."

"Thanks," said Harley as she relaxed a little.

"Now, how about you tell me what's going on." Spence sat back down and leaned back in his chair.

"Well, not much to tell. Met Todd years ago. We were both military brats, I guess you could say. My dad was military, stationed in Texas at the time, as was his. Lost track of him after we moved but ran into him years later at a bar in Iowa where I was working. Finally went out with him one night a few months back. He was a Harley rider. He'd had too much to drink and he ran a car off the road and then didn't stop to see if anybody was hurt or not."

"Was anybody hurt?"

"Yeah, the driver. Driver's side of the car hit a tree. Found out later the guy was in a coma and died a few weeks ago."

"That's too bad."

"I would agree on that one. Anyway, he didn't stop and I was on the back of his bike. When he finally let me off, I went to the police and to make a long story short, he seems to not want me around to testify against him. They picked him up for leaving the scene and failing to render aid, but he bailed out. I filed for a no-contact order. Not that a piece of paper would help a whole lot but at least I could have him arrested if he showed up."

"Good move on your part. Now, you won't have to worry about him for a while. He'll be moved to Tuscaloosa for a bit and then sent back

114

to Iowa and will probably get to spend some time behind bars for a few years."

"Thank you. That makes me feel better."

"Listen though, next time you move out of a state where you have a no-contact order, take a copy of it to the clerk in the town where you are. That way the local police know there's the possibility of trouble if the person shows up. It'll just keep you safer."

"Thanks, I never thought about letting you know. Guess I've just always looked out for myself. My dad saw to that," said Harley as she laughed. "Sent me to karate lessons so I could beat the crap out of any guys who messed with me in case he wasn't around."

"Good move on your dad's part. But you need to let us help look out for you, too."

"Thanks, Sheriff, I'll do that."

"Name's Spence. Cody tells me you're related to Tilly Swanson."

"Yes. She was my Aunt. I inherited her house. Fixing it up to sell it."

"Nice old house. With a little TLC it would be a great place to call home."

"Yeah, it's a nice place. It'll make a great home for somebody."

"Well, we'd sure love to have you stay on here. Tilly was a great lady. She loved Shady Rivers and given a little time, you might like it, too."

"We'll see," said Harley, "Is there anything else you need from me?"

"Just a few signatures on some paperwork. It'll take me a little bit to get it all typed up so how about if you stop back by in the morning and I'll have it all ready for you."

"Sure, I can do that," said Harley as she stood up to leave.

"You rest easy. He's locked up tighter a drum. You enjoy the rest of your day now," said Spence as he stood up and walked her to the door.

"Thanks, I will."

"You tell that Cody he better not be a minute late today. Abby's fixing me some fried green tomatoes for supper tonight and I like 'em hot from the skillet," said Spence as he smiled.

"Fried green tomatoes?"

"Don't tell me you've never eaten fried green tomatoes?" said Spence as he opened the door.

"No, never have."

"Girl, next time you're over to Katy's, get yourself an order of her fried green tomatoes. They're so good they'd bring tears to a glass eye."

"Well, now, I'll just have to stop in for lunch and give it a try then," said Harley as she walked out the door. "Thanks, Spence."

"You're welcome, ma'am. See you in the morning."

"'Kay," said Harley as she closed the door behind her and stepped off the sidewalk onto the street. It was definitely going to be a scorcher today. The humidity already felt as though she could cut it with a knife. She headed for Hale's Grocery. She understood from Katy that was where the local post office was and she wanted to be sure her own mail would be delivered to Aunt Tilly's address.

Harley spent the rest of the day wondering through the quaint little shops in Shady Rivers.

Everywhere she went, someone stopped her on the street, giving her a big hug and usually some words of reassurance that they were so glad that brute of a man didn't have a chance to get her off by herself. Why, there's no telling what he'd have done.

At each store she walked into, the proprietor or proprietress hurried out from behind their counter or stopped whatever they were doing to give her a hug and a little reassurance.

By the time evening had settled in, Harley felt as though she'd been hugged by all ninety-nine Shady Rivers' residents and possibly a few who weren't.

It was a good feeling. One she'd never had before. She liked this town and its people. She felt like she belonged here, as though they were all one big happy family. But that thought was quickly overtaken by another one as she realized she could never stay here. Not with Cody living here, too. She already felt something where Cody was concerned, and she couldn't take the chance of letting her heart be ripped out of her chest again. That old familiar feeling of not belonging, not being worthy enough hit her full force.

Maybe she should just cut her losses and let the real estate company sell the house and all its contents as is, once Cody's lease ran out. She could just get right back on her Harley and ride off, leaving her problems behind.

But, riding off to parts unknown hadn't gotten rid of her problems in the past and if she really faced the truth, she knew it wouldn't get rid of them now either.

No, running wasn't an option this time. She liked this town. Aunt Tilly had liked this town and she knew why. Because everyone here was loved and treated like family. Everyone belonged. No one got left behind while their mother sat in some little sidewalk cafe in France. But what was she going to do about Cody?

She'd just have to steer clear of him until his lease ran out is all. That wouldn't be so hard to do. He slept days while she was up and about, and he worked nights while she was sleeping so that was good. She really wouldn't have to see him at all. She could plan her days accordingly.

Once his lease ran out, she wouldn't see him at all. If she never saw him again, that would be just fine with her. He could have his one-night stands or whatever that poor unsuspecting young woman had been, and she could have a quaint little town that seemed like all the family she would ever need.

CHAPTER TWENTY-SIX

Harley sat on the gazebo, nestled in the town square, watching people gather at the other end. There was a stage of sorts labeled *'The Pickin' Porch.'* She'd seen it on her walks around the town. People were now gathering with lawn chairs and blankets to throw on the ground to sit on.

On stage, a few musicians were tuning instruments getting ready to play. But this band was not like the ones she was used to. These were old timey instruments to her. Banjos, fiddles and other instruments she wasn't familiar with.

Harley watched from her vantage point on the gazebo as Honey Malone stepped out of her hat shop and locked the door before heading across the street to the square carrying a small picnic basket with her.

"Hey darlin'," said Honey.as she stepped up on the gazebo. "Mind if I join you for a bit?"

"Not at all. I'd enjoy a little company."

"Well, I don't know how much 'company' I'll be after working all day but let me pour us a drink from my thermos and we'll both feel better in no time at all," said Honey as she sat down on one of the chairs and opened her basket. "I like to have a mimosa in the evenings. Helps one relax."

"Didn't have too many calls for mimosas in the bar I used to work in. It was more like a beer and whiskey place," laughed Harley.

"Then you're in for a treat. A little champagne, a little freshly-squeezed orange juice, what could be better?" said Honey as she handed a paper cup to Harley.

Harley took a sip.

"Oh, that is good."

"Stop by my shop anytime. I usually have some in the fridge in the back and if not, it only takes a minute to make a batch."

"I was admiring some of the hats in your window display today."

"Did you see something you like?" asked Honey as she sipped from her own cup.

"I'm not much into hats. I'm more of a helmet girl," said Harley as she laughed.

"Well, bring your helmet by and we can always have fun sprucing it up if you want," said Honey as she grinned.

"Do many of the women around here wear hats like that?"

"Just on Sundays. But, I sell a lot of hats to New York designers and to a ton of ladies for the Kentucky Derby."

"Wow. How'd you get hooked up with New York from down here."

"Well, when I was still in high school, they had this contest at the state fair here. It was to see who could make the best Kentucky Derby style hat. I've always loved playing dress-up, so I entered the contest. Won first place, too. Then some newspaper reporter was doing a piece on state fairs and put a picture of my hat in the article. One of the New York designers got hold of a copy of the article and the rest, as they say, is history. I started getting orders for hats, then I started getting orders from women who were wanting a fabulous hat creation to wear to the Kentucky Derby. And I've been making hats ever since."

"That's absolutely awesome."

"It is. I get to do what I love and earn a living at it, too. That's the best kind of work to have. I've always been told to figure out what your passion is and do that. So I guess that'd be my advice to anybody. Find your passion and do it. What about you? What do you do?"

"Nothing in particular. A little of this and a little of that, I guess. Never had roots in one place long enough to do much of anything. I've bartended and played waitress. Right now, I'm doing a few repairs to my Aunt's house, getting ready to sell it. Once I get that done, I'll probably find some place to go," said Harley as she sipped at her drink.

"Well, whenever you do decide to settle someplace, Shady Rivers isn't a bad place to settle. People here treat you like one of the family."

"I've noticed that," said Harley.

"Your Aunt Tilly was one of my teachers."

"I don't think there's anybody in town who didn't have her as a teacher," laughed Harley. "Seems everybody I've talked to was her student at one time or another."

"That's probably the gospel truth," laughed Honey. "She was a sweet lady. Oh, listen, they're starting to play," said Honey as she turned toward the sound.

"I recognize the banjo, the fiddle and the guitar. Do you know what the other instruments are?" asked Harley.

"Oh, sure, Elmer there, he's the end one on the right side. He's playing a hammered dulcimer. He hand-makes them himself over there in his shop next to mine. The Sweet Strings Dulcimer Shoppe. And the lady next to him, that's Mrs. Becky Forsyth, from the bakery. She plays mountain dulcimer. That's her daughter, Elli, next to her on guitar. Then Mel Tuckerman on banjo. Joe South there on fiddle and his son, Mike, next to him on juice harp and jug. Holding up the other end is Skeeter Johnson on washtub bass."

"Is that what that thing is?"

"Yeah, he made it himself. Wait'll he gets down on that thing. You're in for a treat," said Honey, "as she stood up. "Oh, and those two young girls stepping up on the stage there are Keara Day on acoustic guitar and Taryn Day on fiddle. They come down every summer to visit family. Come on, let's go join the crowd before all the good spots are taken."

"All these flowers sure smell good," said Harley as she stepped off the gazebo.

"There's nothing that smells better than the south. Mimosas, that's those pink powder puff looking trees, magnolia, gardenias, wild Jasmin and honeysuckles. That's the smells of a southern night. Nothing finer," said Honey.

"I'd have to agree with you on that. It definitely smells heavenly," said Harley as she took a deep breath inhaling the flower-scented odor of the night breeze as they walked along the path.

CHAPTER TWENTY-SEVEN

Harley awoke early. She hoped she could slip downstairs to shower, and get back upstairs before Cody came in.

She quickly gathered her shampoo, bathing soap and towel and headed to Cody's bedroom. It was too bad the hall bath was only a half bath. Then, she wouldn't have to go into Cody's bedroom at all.

Scurrying into the bath, she stopped short at the sight of his clothes laying all over the floor.

"What a slob," she said out loud to herself.

"I am not," replied Cody from behind the shower door.

Harley screamed.

"Hey, calm down, it's just me. No spiders, see," he said as he slid back the shower door while holding the towel over his pertinent parts.

"Shut that damn door!" yelled Harley.

"What, you don't like the view or something?" asked Cody with a grin.

"No! I don't," she yelled back.

"Well, then, why'd you come barging into my bathroom?" he asked.

"I was going to take a shower and get the hell out of here before you got home."

"Yeah, about that," said Cody, "I haven't seen you in about four days now. So, what gives? You avoiding me for some reason?"

"No, I'm just trying to stay out of your way. Not cramp your style, so to speak," said Harley as she turned her back to him so she wouldn't have to imagine what was underneath that towel. Although she didn't have to imagine, she'd seen everything after the spider incident and getting that image out of her mind was definitely impossible. The man was well equipped to say the least.

Now, she stood facing the bathroom mirror, his naked masculine physique still on display. She cast her gaze downward.

"My style, my style. What style would that be?" he asked.

"You know, the kind where frat boys put socks on the doorknob as a signal."

"What? What the hell are you talking about? I haven't put any socks on any doorknobs," said Cody as he stepped out of the shower next to her.

"Yeah, well, that's the problem. I have no idea when you're, ah, entertaining, so to speak," said Harley as she tried to move further away but the bathroom didn't leave much space between them.

"Listen, sweetheart, I don't have any idea what you're talking about here with socks and doorknobs and entertaining but if you'd care to explain it to me ..."

"You know perfectly well what I'm talking about. You had a, a, a friend over the other morning. I came downstairs and there you two

126

were asleep on the couch. I could have walked in earlier or later for that matter and God knows what I would have seen."

"What? Hold on there, sweetheart. Is that what this avoiding me thing is all about? You saw me asleep on the couch with Vinny," said Cody as he began to laugh.

"It's not funny," said Harley as she turned and socked him in the stomach with her balled up fist.

"Umpfh!" groaned Cody as he bent over grabbing his stomach. "Hold on just a minute, now. Don't go beatin' me up just 'cause I slept with my cousin!"

"Your cousin, your cousin, you slept with your cousin! Ewwww!"

"No. Not slept with as in slept with. Slept with as in we were watching a movie and fell asleep. No big deal. She lives in T-Town with her boyfriend and sometimes she comes down for a visit."

"Oh," said Harley as she stepped sideways toward the bathroom door. "I'll just go back upstairs until you finish in here." She grabbed at the doorknob.

Cody's hand landed on the door preventing her from opening it.

"Not so fast, sweetheart," he said.

Harley looked up at him, and saw the grin spreading across his face and dancing in his eyes.

"What?" she said.

"I do believe you were jealous."

"Jealous! Jealous! Hell no," she said as she pushed, unsuccessfully, at the hand holding the doorway. "Let me out of here."

"Nope. Not till you fess up. You were jealous and we both know it," said Cody as he pushed a stray hair behind her ear. "You know, you have the cutest little ear."

His finger traced from the top of her ear down to her earlobe. He felt Harley's breath catch as he closed the small space between them. Dropping the towel from his other hand, he wrapped his arm around her waist and pulled her in to him. She fit perfectly.

"Cody, I—"

"Shhhh, sweetheart, I want to kiss you."

Harley stood looking at his lips, remembering the feel of them and wanting to feel them again. Her breath came in quick spurts as her heartbeat quickened its pace. A tingle shot through her body landing at her core and she knew at that moment she'd fallen hopelessly in love with Cody Dalton. What was she going to do now?

Cody's lips touched hers as he pressed her against the bathroom counter with his body. He wanted this woman like he had never wanted another. There was just something about her that ignited his desire like no other.

Cody reached down to her bottom and lifted her up, her legs locking around his waist.

"Sweetheart," he mumbled between his lips kissing hers, "unless you stop me now—"

"I don't think I want to stop you," she said before he could finish his sentence. She had wanted this man since that first day. There had just been something about him. He was sweet and sensitive and who else would ever have taken the time to spend Christmas with her in July. She wanted whatever he could give her and if her

128

heart was broken into a million pieces later, she'd just have to deal with it then. Right now, she wanted what was being offered.

Cody opened the bathroom door with one hand and carried her to his bed.

Laying her down gently, he fell on top of her, as one knee fell between her legs. He continued kissing her lips before sliding downward to kiss her neck and the top of her breasts.

Reaching down underneath the oversized t-shirt she'd slept in, with one hand he worked his way upward to her breasts. She moaned as he cupped one in his hand and tweaked at the nipple. He pulled the shirt up high enough to allow his tongue to caress the hardened nipple.

"Let me get you out of these clothes," he said, as he raised himself enough to pull the shirt upward and over her head. Reaching down he pulled at her panties, sliding them down her hips and dropping them to the floor beside her shirt. He quickly reached up to his nightstand drawer and grabbed a condom.

A moment later, his hand returned to her breast and his lips found hers. Her lips parted for him and he took the kiss deeper. Trailing kisses down the side of her neck and across the top of her breast, he felt the fingers of her one hand clutching his hair while her other grabbed at his back. She tasted sweet. He trailed one hand downward to her core, sliding his fingers between the folds.

Harley moaned, her fingernails biting into the flesh of his back. She wanted this man. She knew she'd wanted him since she first saw him. There was no logical explanation as to why she felt that way. No other man had affected her like that. There was just something about Cody that made her soul sing.

Cody felt as if someone had just opened up the universe, and everything there was to know about life had been revealed to him in that one touch. He knew she was the only woman he would ever be satisfied with and she would be the center of his life for as long as he lived. Nothing would ever be right unless she was by his side. How had that happened to him? She had come riding up Main Street on a Harley and his life had been changed forever.

Cody kissed his way down to her core, worshiping her body with his tongue and fingers until he felt her orgasm hit her so hard she screamed from the sheer power of it.

Then, kissing his way back up her body, he moved over the top of her positioning himself before sliding into her. He wanted that moment to last forever. Gathering her tighter in his embrace, his only thought was more. I need more.

They moved in unison, generating a heat together that threated to consume them both and in the same instant together the fire burned out of control and took them over the top, leaving them both breathless and exhausted.

Cody knew in that moment nothing in his world would ever be the same again.

"What have you done to me?" he whispered.

After years of avoiding men and the complications that came with them, all Harley could think of at that moment was mine. All mine. She would never be able to get enough of this man.

CHAPTER TWENTY-EIGHT

"Imagine such a shameful disgrace!" said Flo as she combed out Agnes' hair.

"I know his mama, whoever she is, is just beside herself with shame," replied Agnes. "I mean, just look at him with those painted up lips and that platinum blonde hair. And nekkid as the day he was born except for them pink spiked heels and that little pink powder puff hiding his tallywhacker. Lawd, have mercy!"

"How'd he ever get into Bryant-Denny Stadium in the first place. Let alone sprawled out there on the fifty-yard line for everybody to see. And what on earth was he doing out there with all that, uh, stuff. Just look at that," said Sandra holding the newspaper closer to get a better look as she sat waiting her turn with Flo.

"What was he doing with that blow-up doll handcuffed to hisself like that?" asked Agnes.

"Lawd, girl, I don't have the foggiest but, if you ask me, he's some kind of pervert for sure," replied Sandra.

"And married to our sweet Nadine, he was," said Flo.

"Yeah, thank goodness, Nadine got herself divorced from that scumbag before this hit the paper. And him with all them wives, I tell you, Flo, that man is just bad news," said Agnes.

"Well, I certainly agree with you there, hon," said Flo, looking toward the door as she heard the jingling of the bell.

"Morning, ladies," said Dixie as she waltzed into the shop with a Cheshire cat eating grin all over her face. "I see you've seen today's paper."

"Can you believe this?" asked Agnes. "What a low life scumbag."

"You took the words right outta my mouth, Agnes," said Dixie as she winked at Flo.

Flo smiled back.

"I mean, really. On the fifty-yard line and dressed like that to boot! He's got that bright red lipstick smeared all over his face and on that blow-up doll's 'Christmas' of all places! I mean, for heaven's sake! Lawd, have mercy," said Agnes.

"Well, all I can say is that doll got the short end of the stick," replied Dixie.

"Did he use that whip on himself or on the doll?" asked Sandra. "You think he's one of them perverts that likes to get his tallywhacker whipped? I've heard they can't get it up unless somebody's beatin' on it like that."

"What you been readin', girl?" asked Dixie.

"Ah, well, you know them magazines at the grocery," stumbled Sandra as her face flushed.

"I'm only teasing you. I see those magazines all the time," said Dixie as she winked at Flo. "Flo, I'm just gonna go put your can of coffee in the back."

"Thanks, hon," said Flo. "Sure appreciate you picking it up for me this morning. I thought I had an extra can back there but guess I must've used it. Just put it over there by the coffee pot. I'll need it later."

"Sure thing."

CHAPTER TWENTY-NINE

After working his night shift then having exhausting sex with Harley, Cody had slept like a baby until two in the afternoon. Harley had pulled the drapes closed to keep the room dark but she'd left him a note to let him know she had gone to the lawyers office over in Tuscaloosa.

After showering and getting dressed, he'd made himself a quick breakfast before heading over to Katy's Kitchen. He was hoping to catch some of the ladies who usually congregated there in the afternoons for pie and gossip.

Today he was in luck. Agnes Moorhead, Gertie Mae Gillespie and Mrs. Becky Forsysth sat at one of the red-checkered tablecloth covered tables in the center of the cafe.

"Well, my goodness, aren't you ladies looking especially gorgeous today!" said Cody as he walked up to the table.

"Well, I s'wanee, but you're just the sweetest thang," said Mrs. Becky. "Now, you just come here and give me a smooch right here," she said pointing to her cheek as she turned it up to him.

"My pleasure, Mrs. Becky," said Cody as he stepped over beside her and placed a kiss on her cheek.

"Now you just sit down here with us and cool off a spell," said Gertie Mae, "It's so hot out there you'll be sweating like a whore in church afore you know it."

"I think you're right on that one, Ms. Gertie, said Cody.

"What'll ya have?" asked Katy as she walked up to the table as Cody pulled out a chair and sat down.

"A big ol' glass of sweet tea," said Cody.

"Comin' right up. How about you ladies? You doing okay?"

"I'm fine," said Gertie as the other two ladies nodded their assent.

"Ladies, I need a little help and I'm thinking you three ladies might be able to help me out."

"Sure hon, you need us to catch one of them there criminal elements?" asked Gertie reaching for her handbag.

"No, no ma'am, it's something a lot more fun than chasing criminals," replied Cody. "Here's what I have in mind.

CHAPTER THIRTY

"You know, Gogh, Ms. Katy is a smart lady," said Bubba as he sat on his couch with his feet propped up rubbing the cat's belly as it lay beside him. "I mean, I just have to figure out this whole Jonette thing. I mean, she was like, like, like, well, I just don't know how to explain it. I mean, as long as I didn't know about her, you know, her, her, well, you know. As long as I didn't know about that I really, really liked her. She was fun. It was like, I mean, we liked the same things and all. You know."

The cat meowed as if answering and licked at its paw.

"Yeah, I know you liked her. That's only 'cause she brung you them treats all the time. But, me, well, I just don't know if I'll ever be able to get around the fact she was a he. I mean that's a pretty big thing to get around, don't ya think?"

The cat jumped down from the couch and headed out to the kitchen. Bubba took the last sip from his coffee cup before following the cat.

"Okay, fellow," he said as he put fresh dried cat food in Van Gogh's bowl and took the carton of milk from the fridge, filled the cat's small milk bowl and placed it in the microwave. A few seconds later, Bubba took the bowl of milk and set it on the floor in front of the cat.

"Okay, boy, I'm off to work. See ya when I get back home. Stay out of trouble today, ya hear," Bubba said as he headed for the front door.

* * *

Flo's door jingled as Agnes came in for her weekly appointment.

"Morning, Agnes," said Flo as she turned the styling chair around for Agnes to sit in.

"Morning, Flo. Have you heard yet?"

Flo had to smile to herself. If there was an ounce of new gossip within fifty miles, Agnes Moorhead knew about it. Agnes had been a telephone switch board operator back in the day and knew people all over the area. Flo could only imagine the hours Agnes still spent gabbing on the phone these days.

"Probably not. So what is it I haven't heard about yet?" Flo swung the styling chair around for Agnes.

After settling herself in the chair, Agnes continued, "Well, remember I was telling you 'bout the Reverend?"

"Don't tell me there's more," said Flo as she draped a plastic cape around Agnes to keep hair clippings from falling on her clothes.

"Yep, sugar, there's more." Agnes swooshed her hand out from under the cape so she could talk better. "Seems Betty Marie has the syphilis, too. Can you believe that? That skanky Reverend done gave his wife the syphilis. She should just cut his tallywacker off like that one lady did, you know that one, what was her name?"

"Bobbitt, Lorena Bobbitt."

"Yeah, that's her. Bless her heart, she performed the only castration heard around the world." Agnes laughed. "More women should do that."

"Well, I have to admit, there are a few guys out there who might deserve it," said Flo as she began to comb out Agnes' hair.

"Oh, don't get me started on that!" said Agnes. "She should have fried it up and fed it to him while she was at it. Say, have you seen that sweet Nadine. I mean, after that scumbag she was married to's picture came out in the paper. I mean him laying out there on the fifty-yard line in that get up and all. That man's a whole truck-load of bricks shy of a load."

Flo looked up as the door jingled again.

"Hey, ya'll," said Honey as she stepped inside. "It's already hotter'n a blister bug in a pepper patch out there."

"It's definitely gonna be a scorcher today," said Flo. "I think you could fry an egg on the sidewalk out there already. There's sweet tea in the back."

"Oh thanks, I could definitely use something cold this morning," Honey said as she headed for the back room. Moments later she returned sipping on a cold glass of tea. "Just wanted to let you know Dixie said seven tonight."

"I'll be there," said Flo.

"See ya then," said Honey as she opened the door. "I'll bring your glass back." Honey closed the door as she stepped outside.

"Whatcha doing at seven?" asked Agnes as she watched Flo clip a stray hair here and there.

"We were thinking about going over to Tuscaloosa to eat and take in a movie," said Flo crossing her fingers behind Agnes' back until she'd finished her sentence, hoping her little untruth wouldn't count against her on judgment day.

"Well, in my younger days, I'd go with you but I'm afraid I'll be in bed by that time, so you'll just have to get along without me," said Agnes oblivious to the fact she hadn't been invited.

* * *

After spending the morning in Tuscaloosa with her attorney, Harley drove into her driveway and parked her motorcycle back inside the barn. Heading outside, she closed the barn door behind her. Seeing movement out of the corner of her eye, she turned just as a gloved hand crushed a rag over her nose and mouth. Darkness crashed into her brain.

CHAPTER THIRTY-ONE

Harley awoke to the coldness around her. Her mind was foggy. Her hands ached, and she tried to move them from over her head, but something prevented it. Her fingers registered something which felt like plastic. Her mind raced trying to remember. The thoughts were there but she couldn't quite grasp onto them.

Then the memory overloaded her brain all at once. Todd. She'd caught a glimpse of his face just before she passed out. Where was she? What had he done to her? More importantly what was he planning to do with her?

How had he gotten out of jail? Sheriff Cartwright had called and told her the Tuscaloosa Police Department had picked him up earlier and would keep him there until he could be transported back to Iowa where he would definitely be spending a little time waiting for his trial.

Where was she? Looking around her surroundings she realized she was in her own basement utility room. Washer, dryer, a few canned goods and a freezer. She began to list what she knew. First, she was lying on a concrete floor. He'd been stupid enough to tie her hands above her head with a zip tie.

No need to panic. Her dad had made darn sure she could protect herself if need be. All those years of studying various martial arts were, hopefully, going to pay off now. She just needed to get her hands free then, whenever he returned, she would unleash the hounds of hell on him. Once she finished with him she'd call Sheriff Cartwright to come haul his ass to jail.

She needed to be as quiet as possible so as not to alert Todd to the fact that she was alert.

Scooting herself up on her butt, she managed to slide herself as close as she could to the water line Todd had tied her to. Twisting her torso into a pretzel, she managed to get one foot close enough to her hands to untie its shoelace and pull it through the zip tie. Then she re-tied it to the other lace on the tennis shoes she wore. Once she was sure it was tied tightly, she began to pedal with both feet and, in less than a minute, she was free. Thank goodness her dad had taught her that little trick when she was six years old.

Quietly, she snuck over to the door, stood with her back to the wall next to the doorknob and waited.

It seemed an eternity had passed before she finally heard movement outside the door. She could tell he must have propped a chair or something against the door from all the noise he was making.

The door opened and Todd stepped inside. Immediately, Harley's leg came up and her foot landed hard in his groin causing him to bend over in pain. She was on his back in less than a

142

second with her arm pulled tightly around his throat choking off his air supply. He tried to reach around to pull her off but within seconds he fell face down on the floor unconscious with Harley still riding his back.

Hearing movement behind her she rolled off Todd and sat staring at Cody as he leaned against the door jam.

"You know," said Harley, as she stood up staring at Cody, "you could have jumped in at any time."

"And risk having you beating the hell out of me while you were whipping his ass. I don't think so. And where the hell did you learn to fight like that anyway?" he said as he walked over to the unconscious man on the floor.

"Master of Martial Arts. Jujitsu, boxing, karate. Just earned my second-degree black belt a few months back."

"Damn, woman, don't ever get pissed at me, okay?" he said as he rolled the guy onto his stomach and put the cuffs on him.

"Just don't do anything to piss me off."

"I'll try to remember that."

Hearing footsteps coming down the stairs toward the basement, Cody turned toward the sound, his hand resting on the butt of his gun.

"Hey Cody," said Spence ducking through the doorway as he entered the small room. "Everything secured here?"

"Yeah, didn't have to do much. Just put the handcuffs on him was all. Just don't ever get on her bad side," Cody said as he nodded toward Harley.

"You okay, Harley?" asked Spence as he looked in her direction.

"Yeah, I'm fine."

"He didn't, uh—"

"No, no, nothing like that. Well, that I'm aware of, anyway. I mean, I don't remember anything from the time he grabbed me out there at the barn until I came to in here."

"What happened when he grabbed you?" asked Spence.

"I had just gotten back home and drove my bike into the barn. I was coming out of the barn and had just shut the barn door and I caught a glimpse of movement and saw Todd's face right before the lights went out."

"And what happened when you came to?"

"Well, I was alone in here. It was dark and my hands were tied. Took me a few minutes to get coherent but then I just kind of assessed the situation. Took me a minute to get my hands untied. Then I just waited for him to show up. I heard him coming and I was over there by the door. When he stepped inside I took him down."

"What'd you do to take him down?" asked Spence.

"Kicked him in the groin then cut off his air supply."

"That would do it," said Spence as he smiled at her. "Oh, hi, Doc, come on in. Harley's going to be your victim for tonight's ride. Take good care of her," said Spence. "Cody, how about if you go with her. You can get the rest of the information on the ride to the hospital."

"Wait a minute. How'd you all know I was in trouble in the first place?" asked Harley.

"Easy," said Cody. "I came home and first thing I notice was the barn door was still open. You must not have gotten it latched. Wind must've blown it all the way open. Didn't seem right to me with you not being anywhere around. Got to looking around and noticed the drag marks on the ground. He must've drug you into the house. I knew something was wrong at that point, so I called Spence, then went looking for you. Found you down here beating the tar out of this guy. And I might say you did a mighty fine job of it, too!"

"Oh," said Harley.

"And I called Doc after Cody here called me. Wanted him here just in case. And don't worry, Harley, I'll see to this guy and he won't be able to get out before trial. He's facing murder charges now. The man in that car died this morning. Add kidnapping charges on top of it and he'll be sent away for a long time."

"Come on," said Cody, let's get you checked over good," said Cody as he walked over to Harley. "You walk okay?"

"Nothing's broken, if that's what you mean," Harley said, "but I'm fine. I don't need to get checked out." She wiped at the dirt on her clothes.

"Humor me. Doc here'll run you over to Tuscaloosa. Let them document every scrape. We want to be sure to give the prosecutor every ounce of info we can."

"Well, if he never sees the light of day that'll be fine with me," said Harley.

"Good. I'm going to need you to come over to the office and file a report on this moron, but you can do it tomorrow. Right now, Doc has the ambulance outside and he'll take you over to Tuscaloosa to get checked out."

"Alright then, the quicker we get this done, the quicker I can get back home," said Harley as she started out the doorway and up the stairs behind Doc Watkins.

Cody smiled to himself. Home was a word he liked to hear her say.

* * *

"You okay," asked Cody as he sat in the back of the ambulance holding onto Harley's hand.

"Yeah, I'm fine. And thanks, for coming with me."

"You're welcome. Listen, I didn't get to thank you for last night and all, I mean—"

"No need to thank me. I seem to have had a little fun, too, you know."

"Well, I was hoping you enjoyed it."

"Actually, I enjoyed it enough, I thought maybe we could do it again sometime."

"Just say the word and I'm your man," said Cody as he leaned over and placed a kiss on her forehead. "Now, you just rest until Doc gets us to the hospital. I'm not leaving your side until that scumbag is outta town for good."

"You don't have to do that. I can take care of myself."

"Yeah, that's obvious, but I thought maybe you'd protect me. Damn woman, but I never want to get on your bad side. You are dangerous. Did you know that?"

"You can thank my dad for that."

"Well, that's one thing he did for you that was right. I've always thought girls should be taught how to fight. I mean, us boys, now, we start fighting with each other by the time we can walk. But girls don't do that kind of thing so most grow up without that benefit. I just think more need to be able to do what you did."

"My daughters will definitely know how to fight."

"Your daughters. You want kids?"

"Yeah, some day. Don't you?"

"I want a ton of them. I want to be able to sit on my front porch and watch 'em playing in the yard on a sunny summer afternoon."

Doc Watkins pulled the ambulance into the emergency bay at the hospital and scurried around to open the door for the emergency team as they hurried out of the door toward the vehicle.

"She's doing okay," said Doc as the team arrived and began taking the gurney Harley was on, out of the back of the ambulance.

"I'm fine," said Harley. "Just got a sore foot from kicking a guy's pride and joy is all." She laughed.

"Good for you, ma'am, but you just lay still and we'll get you inside and check everything out," replied one of the team.

CHAPTER THIRTY-TWO

Harley had slept late. She hadn't realized just how much the events from the day before had exhausted her.

Now that she'd gotten her dad's insurance money, she'd at least have enough to live on comfortably for a year or more until the rest of her inheritance was settled.

Today, she would get dressed, head over to Katy's Kitchen for breakfast and decide what she wanted to do about Aunt Tilly's house. She could fix it up and stay right here with these people who were fast becoming her friends, or she could sell it and move on.

Moving on just sounded tiring. Maybe she just needed to find a job here and set down her own roots where she might find a path to her own family. Aunt Tilly had loved it here and the people in this town seemed to have loved her, too. Harley wanted that kind of family.

* * *

Harley walked through the town square and sat on the gazebo step. This little town was certainly peaceful. The scent of gardenias wafted through the air. She watched as a lone bison walked around the corner of the Sheriff's Office and headed toward the park. *Tiny.* Or at least she hoped that was who it was. This thing looked huge as it walked across the park and helped itself to a drink of water from the wading pool around the wishing well fountain. She watched as it drank its fill then looked around before it headed in her direction.

Harley sat perfectly still. She'd never encountered a bison, large or small, up this close and personal. The animal walked up in front of her and stood still as though it was trying to decide whether or not she was worth his time.

Tiny slowly moved closer and then closer still. Harley felt his hot breath on her face. Slowly she raised her hand and rubbed the side of his face.

"Well, hello there," she said as she continued to rub. "You must be Tiny."

Tiny's tongue came out and licked her face. He snortled as if to say 'yep, that's me,' turned an ambled toward the other end of the square.

Harley watched as he met up with Gertie Mae, who appeared to give him something to eat. Harley had heard the big bison had a penchant for fried apple pies and assumed that's what Gertie Mae had given him. A few minutes later, he continued on his way.

Gertie Mae continued on her way up the walkway leading to the gazebo.

"Good morning," said Gertie as she got close enough to see Harley sitting on the steps.

"Good morning, Gertie, how are you this morning?"

150

"I'm doing just fine, but how are you sweetheart? I heard about that evil man. Good gracious amighty, but you can't get away from scum like that till you put 'em in their graves. Now, me, I got my ol' daddy's revolver, a Colt .45, right here in my purse. I never know when I'm gonna need it."

"You carry a gun in your purse?"

"Well, fer sure. Don't you?"

"No. Don't usually even carry a purse," said Harley as she smiled at Gertie. " Is it loaded?"

"Well, it'd be rather useless now if it wasn't," replied Gertie with a laugh. "So, tell me now, just how'd you get away from that mean man then?" asked Gertie as she carefully sat down beside Harley.

"I just kicked him where it counts," said Harley as she winked at Gertie.

"You mean you kicked in him the tallywacker?" asked Gertie as she sat back in surprise.

"Yep, that'd be the spot."

"Lawd have mercy, girl!" Gertie began to laugh, a tiny giggle at first which erupted into a full belly laugh before long.

Harley watched a moment before erupting into laughter herself at the dear little ol' lady who was obviously enjoying that thought.

Gertie laughed so hard, her purse slid out of her lap and onto the ground. Her small bottle of cannabis oil slid out and rolled onto the ground in front of Harley.

"Ladies," said Cody as he walked up from beside them and stood with his hands on his hips in front of Gertie Mae.

"Hey, Cody," said Harley, trying to contain her laughter.

"Harley," he nodded. "Ladies, I'm going to assume neither one of you happens to own that little bottle laying there because, if you did, I'd be obliged to haul you off to jail because it's illegal to buy it or sell it, unless, of course, you're using it for medicinal purposes in which case you'd need a doctor's prescription."

"Well who was the damn fool who came up with that law? You can use it for medicinal purposes. You just can't buy it or sell it. Now what sense does that make? If ya can't buy it, how the hell are ya supposed to get it? I mean for medicinal purposes and all," said Gertie Mae.

"I think that's the whole point, Ms. Gertie. Seems the powers that be just don't want you getting your hands on it. So, tell you what. See, I know you're a fine, upstanding citizen here in Shady Rivers so I'm going to entrust this little bottle of cannabis oil to you. Now, what I want you to do is to put it in your purse there until you can get home with it. Once you get home with it, I want you to flush it down the drain so none of the kids around here come across it," said Cody as he picked up the bottle and handed it to Gertie as he winked in her direction.

"Well, I just better stop lollygagging around and amble on towards home so's I can get rid of this evil stuff fer ya then," said Gertie as she took the small bottle from Cody's hand.

"I'd be much obliged to you for helping me out, Ms. Gertie," he said as he offered his hand to help her up.

Cody and Harley watched as Gertie Mae shuffled off in the direction of her home. As she got to the far corner of the town square, Tiny came from the direction of Smith & Son's Garage and followed close behind her.

"I swear that little lady never ceases to amaze me. Who'd have thought she'd be one to break the law like that?" asked Cody.

"Do you know she carries a loaded gun?" asked Harley as she scooched over to allow Cody to sit down beside her.

"Yep, carries it everywhere with her and even goes to church with her twice on Sundays," said Cody as he sat down on the step beside her.

"To church. She carries a Colt 45 in her purse to church on Sundays." Harley laughed.

"Yep, and she knows how to use it, too. That woman can shoot out a snake's eye a mile up river."

"What the hell does that mean?" asked Harley cocking her head sideways at Cody.

Cody laughed. "Means she's a sharpshooter. Just don't mess with her and her guns."

"Guns? As in more than one?"

"That woman has an arsenal at her house. You should take a tour sometime. It's amazing. She's got one of the first Winchester Model 1873's off the assembly line. Belonged to her Grandpappy's Grandpappy or some Grandpappy somewhere down the line."

"Wow. That's amazing. Just looking at her, you'd never think such a tiny woman would even be able to carry a gun much less know how to use one."

"Yeah, well don't let her size fool ya. She's a force to be reckoned with for sure."

"Tell me something. At Katy's the other day, everybody pulled out guns. I think every female in the place had one. Does everybody down here have guns?"

"Well, sweetheart, it's like this. Down here, you never know when you're going to step out in your yard and find a copperhead or a rattlesnake."

"You're kiddin' me, right?"

"Heck, sometimes you find them inside your house. Then there's bobcats and such, too. Lot of people around here hunt for food. You know, deer, rabbits and such. Down here, you just need to be able to take care of yourself. Heck, kids around here are taught how to shoot a gun before they can walk. Kids spend a lot of time outdoors around here. Hunting, building forts in the woods and such. So they need to be able to protect themselves if necessary."

"Well, I suppose so with things slithering all over the place."

"Now, on occasions, a two-legged varmint comes sniffing around these parts and well, most of 'em learn in a hurry what happens to the criminal element around here."

"Yeah, I saw."

"Say, how about if we pick up some breakfast-to-go from Katy's and head out to Aunt Tilly's valley and watch some honey bees?" Cody stood up offering his hand to Harley.

"You know, that sounds nice. I think that's a wonderful idea," she replied as she took hold of his hand pulling herself up from the step.

After grabbing breakfast-to-go from Katy's, they headed out to the valley. Later, her stomach satisfied, Harley lay back on the blanket Cody had taken from his truck and spread out for them amongst the flowers.

It was so peaceful here, underneath the shade tree, watching the honey bees and butterflies pollenate the blossoming flowers. She could definitely do without the heat and humidity but here on the top of the hill the gentle breeze helped.

This slower paced lifestyle wasn't bad at all. Aunt Tilly was on to something here. This, being here, seemed to feed her spirit and that was something she could not ever remember feeling. She'd lived a lifetime of chaos. Always on the move, running. Running from something or running to something made no difference. The problem was it was just geography. It never changed who she was. It only changed the view outside her window. That scared little girl who was so bad her mother left her was still there inside her.

Well, she wanted a better life. Better than the one she'd been born into. Other moms didn't leave their babies. Why had hers?

Maybe she'd been looking at it all wrong all these years. Maybe she hadn't done something so bad after all. Maybe, just maybe, it was her mother's own fault. Could it be something as simple as the mother gene just wasn't included in the package that was her mother?

"It's not your fault, you know," said Cody as he lay back on the blanket beside her.

"What's not my fault?" said Harley as she rolled onto her side to face him.

"What you're thinking," he said as he reached over and pushed a stray strand of hair back behind her ear.

"And what is it I'm thinking?"

"About your mom and her leaving and all," he said as he lifted her chin to get a better view of her face. "Look at me, Harley."

She raised her gaze to his face.

"You did nothing wrong. You were just a kid. Your mother just had a wire loose somewhere. It was all her fault, not yours. It wouldn't have mattered if she'd had just one kid or ten kids, she still would have left. You didn't do a single thing to cause her to leave."

"For the first time in my life, I was just thinking that. Maybe it wasn't me."

"No, sugar, it wasn't you at all," he said as he put his arms around her and pulled her close. "You deserved better. It was just that she couldn't give you better. I hope, someday, you can really see that, but until that day comes you just keep telling yourself it wasn't your fault because you did absolutely nothing wrong."

"Thank you. I'm not sure how you always seem to know what I need but thank you."

Cody kissed her forehead as he rolled her onto her back. His lips found hers and he tenderly kissed her.

"Come on," he said as he jumped up and pulled her up with him.

"What are we doing?" she said.

Cody grabbed her hand and pulled her along with him as he ran down the hill, laughing.

"We're going wading in the creek," he said as they stopped on the creek's bank. "Pull off your shoes and jump in."

"It's not deep is it?" she asked as she bent to remove her shoes.

"Nope. You can see the bottom there."

156

Cody pulled off his shoes and stepped off the bank into the water. It felt cold against his skin. He held his hands up to Harley as she gingerly stepped off the bank and dipped the toes of one foot into the stream.

"Oh, that's cold," she said pulling her foot back out.

Cody released her hands and grabbed her around the waist, picking her up and holding her against his body as he began to lower her toward the water.

"No, no, Cody, don't. That water's cold!" she yelled.

"I'll get you warm," he said as her body slid down the length of his until her face was inches from his.

She wrapped her legs around his waist and lowered her lips to his. She wanted this man. Right here, right now. She thrust her tongue inside his mouth and tasted him. She had to have more. She wanted to feel his skin against hers and she wanted the pleasure she knew he could give her.

Her hands combed through this hair and her lower region could feel the hardness of him through his jeans. She wanted his hardness inside of her making her drunk with pleasure.

One hand found his shirt front and she slid her hand inside the neck opening and caressed his collar bone. It wasn't enough. Tugging at the opening, she felt the button give and her hand immediately found a patch of chest hair. She wanted to taste every inch of him.

Cody tasted the sweetness of her kiss and felt his desire swell. He turned, holding her still clinging around his waist, and walked out of the stream and laid her down on the ground.

"I'm sorry I don't have a blanket here," he whispered, his lips barely lifting from hers.

Her hands tore at his shirt, pushing it from his shoulders. She noticed the empty heart tattoo on his left arm but quickly turned her gaze to what he was doing.

"Here, let me," he said as he raised himself above her and quickly discarded the shirt. Unsnapping his jeans, he quickly pulled them, along with his tighty-whities, off in one quick movement, tossing them aside as he rolled his nakedness over her.

Kissing his way down her neck, he pulled her t-shirt above her breasts and kissed at her nipples through the lacy material of her pink bra while he pulled the straps down her shoulders. Unhooking it from the front, he laid it back and took a nipple into his mouth. She tasted a little sweet and a little salty and he liked that. Unsnapping her jeans, he pulled them and the pink panties she wore down her legs and added them to the clothes already in a pile beside them.

Returning to her lips, his tongue found hers and began to dance. She answered each thrust with her own ravenously deep thrust. Her legs entwined around his waist as he positioned himself over her nakedness.

"Ready?" he whispered, not wanting to take things too fast for her.

Harley groaned as if frustrated because he wasn't going fast enough.

"You make me crazy," said Cody as he drove into her wetness. He kissed her swollen lips and thrust his tongue inside her deliciously soft mouth. Pushing harder into her lusciousness, he could barely breathe as he felt her center tighten around his hardness. He caught the soft skin of her neck with his teeth as he shoved all the way in.

Harley cried out as her back arched. Her nails dug into his back and he stabbed into her over and over until he felt her orgasm start. He wanted his hardness deeper inside her. This woman did things to him. He could hardly breathe as he kissed her furiously as his pumps grew faster and every muscle in his body tightened until they both collapsed in sheer pleasure.

Minutes later Cody rolled off her onto the ground beside her.

Glancing over at her face, he saw she was smiling a lazy, sated smile. He raised himself up onto his elbows and looked down at her.

"I take it you enjoyed that," said Cody.

"I most certainly did," she said with a grin spreading across her face.

"I'm glad. Must say it was rather enjoyable for me, too."

Cody felt a connection to this woman and the promise of something more wonderful to come.

Harley slid her fingers up his chest and rested them on his collarbone momentarily before trailing them down his arm, tracing the outline of the heart tattoo she'd seen there.

Cody lay back beside her. "Look, that cloud there. What's it look like to you?"

"A dog."

"Yeah, that's what I see, too. Did you ever lay out in your yard and watch the clouds float by?"

"No. Lived on base most of the time. Too many lights to see the sky."

"Look at that one," he said as he pointed upward."

"They look so soft. Kinda like a big fluffy pillow."

"Always wondered what it would be like to sit on top of one."

"Wouldn't that be fun!"

They lapsed into a peaceful silence.

"Would you have supper with me tonight?" Cody asked minutes later, as they lay watching the cloud formations float overhead.

"I think I could arrange that, but I'll have to clear my busy schedule, of course, but I'm sure the President can rearrange his schedule to meet with me another day."

"You'd do that for me?" Cody laughed.

"Anybody that can make me feel the way you do definitely gets special treatment. So, yes, I'll cancel all my other plans just for you," she said as she laughed and rolled back on top of him, kissing him on the lips.

"Mmmmmmmm," said Cody, "you keep this up and I know what's gonna happen."

"I have all day," said Harley as she smiled down at him.

CHAPTER THIRTY-THREE

Harley had enjoyed a wonderfully lazy day with Cody. They'd spent the morning skinny dipping and having sex before throwing their clothes back on and heading to Katy's for a quick lunch. Afterwards they'd returned to skinny dipping and more sex all afternoon.

Now, with evening close by, she slid into her jeans and t-shirt before slipping on her sandals and heading down the stairs to meet Cody. He'd gone to pull his pickup out of the barn and up to the front of the house. Since it was hot out, he'd told her to wait inside where she'd stay cool until he got the truck cooled a bit.

Hearing a knock on the door, Harley went to open it. Just as she turned the knob she heard singing. The strains from *Jingle Bells* floated to her ears.

"What the hell?" she asked as she opened the door.

Cody stood in front of the door with a Christmas wreath in his hand. In the yard behind him, stood eight people, some dressed in elf suits while others were dressed as various Christmas

161

renditions of Santa, Mrs. Santa, and even three wise men, singing.

"I know roses are customary but I thought, under the circumstances, you might like this more," said Cody as he held out the wreath.

"Oh my God, what have you done?" whispered Harley as tears rimmed her eyes.

"The other night," said Cody, "at the hospital, as you were filling out the paperwork, I happened to notice that today was your birthday. Me and three of the ladies there had been planning a Christmas in July party for you since you'd never had one and well, we just decided to move it up. So Merry Christmas and Happy Birthday, Harley." He leaned in and kissed her on the cheek.

Harley jumped into his arms and kissed his lips. The singers began a rousing rendition of *Santa Claus is Coming to Town* as Mel Tuckerman pulled a decorated horse drawn sleigh from around the corner of the house and stopped in front of the porch steps.

"Oh my gosh, is that Mel Tuckerman in a top hat and coat?" whispered Harley.

Mel jumped down, doffed his hat, swung it in front of him as he bowed and said "Madam, your sleigh awaits."

"Oh my gosh," whispered Harley, "you did this for me."

"With the help of a few friends," Cody replied. "Shall we?"

"I get to ride in a Christmas sleigh?" whispered Harley.

The singers began singing *Joy to the World* as they gathered around behind it.

"You look positively stunning, Mel," said Harley as he offered his hand to help her into the carriage.

"Thank you, Miss, and a Merry Christmas to you," Mel replied as he winked at her.

"Merry Christmas to you, too, Mel."

Harley seated herself as Cody climbed into the carriage beside her. Reaching into the bottom of the carriage, Cody pulled a blanket up over their laps.

"Christmas is supposed to be cold but since it's July, we're not going to be able to stand this blanket for long," said Cody as he tucked it in around them. "But it's not a sleigh ride without a blanket to keep the cold out."

"This is absolutely perfect, Cody. I've never—"

"Just sit back and relax. The best is yet to come."

"Oh this is the best I could have ever hoped for. This is just, it's just, it's just Christmas."

Mel started the horses at a slow pace allowing the singers to keep up. Twenty minutes later, the sleigh turned the corner onto Main Street. Moments later they were passing Hale's Grocery.

Harley looked ahead. There were twinkling lights lighting up the storefronts along the way. The store windows displayed Christmas decorations and things. The trees and bushes in the town square were lit up and the gazebo was stunning. She could see tiki torches burning around the outside perimeter.

"Oh my gosh, oh my gosh, Christmas! I've never ..." Harley stood up in the carriage to get a better view. "This is just ..." Tears ran down

Harley's cheeks. She turned to Cody as she sank back onto the buggy seat. "I cannot even begin to tell you what this means to me."

"You don't have to, Harley. I can't begin to imagine what it must have been like for you as a kid to never have Christmas and for that I'm truly sorry."

Mel pulled the sleigh up next to the sidewalk close to the gazebo.

"Come on," said Cody, "I promised you some supper. Cody jumped down from the sleigh and reached up grabbing Harley by the waist and lifted her down.

"Thanks, Mel," he said as he took Harley by the elbow and began ushering her toward the gazebo. "I'll call when we're ready to leave."

"Okie doke," said Mel as he turned back to the horses. "Gitty up now, you two." He jiggled the reins slightly and the two horses began shuffling forward. The group of singers trailed along behind heading toward the Pickin' Porch at the other end of the Square as their beautiful rendition of *Silent Night* floated across the night air.

"This is beautiful," said Harley stepping up onto the gazebo. She loved the tiki torches casting an amber glow over the darkness. A table, covered with a white tablecloth, was lit with a single candle surrounded by green holly and red berries sitting in the middle of it. Dim Christmas lights hung around the inside roof of the gazebo. Musicians, who'd been sitting on the Pickin' Porch picked up the song of the carolers as they approached, and Harley could hear the strains of *Deck the Halls* as the musicians kicked in.

"How in the world did you do all this? I mean not only is the whole town decorated but you've got carolers and musicians ..."

"Like I said, I had help. When I told Agnes, Gertie Mae and Mrs. Beck that you'd never had a Christmas before, they thought that was an absolute sin. They took it from there and the whole town got behind the idea of Christmas in July. So, now they've decided to have Christmas in July every year starting on your birthday and lasting for a whole week," replied Cody as he pulled the chair out for Harley. After she was seated he walked around to his own seat and continued. "When you want something done around here, all you have to do is ask either Agnes Moorhead, Gertie Mae Gillespie or Mrs. Becky Forsysth and it'll get done. I just happened to ask all three of 'em and they took care of the rest. It's a wonder the road from here to Tuscaloosa isn't decorated, too."

"Have you driven that way today?" laughed Harley.

"You may have a point there," said Cody as he uncorked the bottle of wine and poured two glasses. Handing a glass to Harley, he lifted his own for a toast. "To Christmas," he said, "and may the delight in your eyes continue throughout every Christmas to come."

"To Christmas," replied Harley as she clinked her glass against his before taking a sip.

"Oh this is good stuff," she said. "What is it?"

"Sassicaia, my favorite and one of the best wines Italy has to offer."

"Well, I'm no wine aficionado but this stuff is good!"

"I'm glad you like it," he said. "But don't get too used to it. It's rather expensive."

Harley noticed as Cody motioned for someone. A waiter appeared in a starched white waiter uniform sporting a Santa Hat carrying two dinner salads.

"Good evening, folks," said Joe South. "Don't know that I've ever been introduced to this purty young lady you got here, Cody." Joe set the two plates in front of them.

"Joe, this is Tilly's niece, Harley. Harley, Joe here owns the garage down yonder. South & Sons. Best darn mechanics this side of the river."

"Pleased to meet you, ma'am," said Joe as he wiped his hand on his pants and shook the hand Harley offered him.

"It's nice to meet you, too."

"Ya'll eat up now. Katy's fixin' the rest of your supper and I'll get it right over here as soon as it's ready," said Joe as he disappeared into the night.

"You heard him," said Cody, "dig in." Cody picked up his fork.

"This looks really good. I'm starving," said Harley as she stuck her fork into the salad for a bite. "I'm just so totally blown away by all of this. No one's ever done anything like this for me before."

"Then I'm glad it was me."

"I think I am, too," said Harley as she looked across the table into Cody's blue eyes.

Cody's fork stopped in mid-air. He wanted to push the dishes to the floor and take her right then and there. This woman did things to him. Nice things. He wanted to feel those things for

166

the rest of his life. Reaching across the table, he took her hand in his.

"Sweetheart, you deserve this. This and so much more," said Cody as he lifted her hand to his lips.

At that moment, the band started a rousing chorus of *Grandma Got Run Over By A Reindeer*.

Harley started to giggle.

"Kinda ruins the moment, doesn't it?"

Harley loved the laughter twinkling in Cody's eyes.

"No, it's just perfect. I happen to like that song."

"Good, then I planned it that way," Cody said as a grin spread across his face.

"Where on earth did you find all those musicians?"

"Oh, that's just a few of the town's folks. That young lady on the fiddle is Taryn Day. She's won a few championship ribbons with her playing."

"I can certainly see why. She's awesome."

"That she is and the young lady next to her on acoustic guitar is her sister, Keara Day. She's got just as many ribbons under her belt. They visit family here every summer. Those two are gonna be playing at the White House someday."

"I can see that happening. They are good!"

"That they are. Now next to Keara on acoustic guitar, too, is Elli Forsyth. Then there's Mike South blowing on that jug. Skeeter Johnson on the washtub bass. Elmer there on the hammered dulcimer; and Mel's on the banjo."

"Does everybody in this town play something?" Harley laughed.

"Not sure about everybody but we do have a passel of musicians around here. Comes from sitting out on the porch on a warm summer night. Somebody starts playing something and eventually their porch and yard are full of pickers and grinners."

"It's like, it's like—"

"One big happy family."

"Yeah, exactly. It's like living in one big happy family."

"That's what folks are around here. Family."

Joe stepped up onto the gazebo with two plates of food.

"Here you are folks. Katy's special dinner for two. Now save some room for her Christmas in July Pie. Boy, it's so good it'll make you wanna slap yo mama!" said Joe as he hurried off towards Katy's Kitchen.

An hour later, supper eaten and pie consumed, Cody poured the last of the wine into their glasses.

"To a wonderful Christmas with a beautiful lady," said Cody. Tipping his glass toward Harley, he took a sip.

"To my first Christmas ever and to the wonderful man who gave it to me," said Harley as she tipped her glass.

"Walk with me over to the fountain there," said Cody.

"I'd love to," said Harley as she began to rise from her seat.

Cody stood and walked around to Harley's side of the table. Pulling her chair back, he took her hand in his as they stepped off the gazebo.

"You have to make a wish," said Cody as they arrived at the fountain, "and once you make the wish you toss in a coin." He reached into his pocket and pulled out change, handing her a dime.

"Okay," said Harley as she took the dime. Standing quietly for a moment, she finally tossed the dime into the water and watched as it floated to the bottom. "What happens to all that money in there?"

"It gets collected and used for the Christmas Artisan Festival event for the townsfolks."

"What's that?"

"Well, in December, all the artists around here have their work on display. We've got crafts of all kinds. Ol' Skeeter blows glass. Elmer makes those hammered dulcimers he plays. Got a few painters over there in the Cat's Meow Artist Studio. People come from all over to buy stuff. So the money just goes to help with advertising expenses."

"Wow, this place never ceases to amaze me."

"You'd really like it here, Harley. I mean, you'd fit right in and all."

"I can certainly understand why Aunt Tilly lived here."

"I think that's why she left you her house. She just knew you belonged here."

"I'm not sure about that. She didn't even know me."

"Knowing Aunt Tilly, I'm thinking she knew more about you than you thought."

"Maybe."

"You know what else I was thinking?"

"What?"

"I was thinking that maybe you'd marry me?"

"What?" asked Harley as she felt a scowl cross her face.

"I said I thought maybe you'd marry me."

"But, you don't know me. I mean, I've only been here in town a short time."

"I know that," said Cody as he took her in his arms. He brushed a stray hair back behind her ear. "And, I know there's something between you and me. I don't know what it is. I can't explain it, but I felt a connection to you that first day and it hasn't gone away. I can give you time. I got all the time in the world. The one thing I don't have is a life if you're not in it."

"But—"

"Sweetheart, I know you don't know a thing about me and all that. I'm willing to give you all the time in the world to get to know me. I'll prove to you that I'm not going anywhere. I'll be right by your side every step of the rest of your life."

"But—"

"Sweetheart, you turn me inside out. I need you in my life. I want you in my life. I want to be the man for you. When you're sad, I want to be the man whose arms you find comfort in. When you're happy, I want to be the man who's there to dance on the tabletops with you. When you're sick, I want to be the man who feeds you chicken soup and puts a cold rag on your forehead. When you need, I want to be the man who fills that need.

Harley reached up and placed her finger against Cody's lips, quietening him. "But Cody, you didn't ask me what I wished for," said Harley.

"Okay, what did you wish for?" he asked as he took her hand and kissed her fingertip.

"I wished that you would love me as much as I love you," said Harley as she gazed into his eyes.

"You love me?"

"How can I not? You gave me Christmas."

"I love you," he said as his lips touched hers, lightly at first and deepening as the world faded around them.

"You two better come up for some air," said Katy as she walked by heading over to join the crowd of listeners enjoying the music on the Porch.

Cody pulled back, his eyes never leaving Harley's, "Hey Katy." Again, his lips found Harley's. "I guess we better join the rest of the crowd," he continued as again he pulled back and stood gazing down into her eyes.

"Yes," she replied.

"Okay, then," he said as he turned slightly taking her hand in his, he started to walk toward the others.

Harley pulled him back.

"No, Cody, I wasn't saying yes to that. I was saying yes to that other thing you were thinking."

"That other thing—" realization dawned. "You mean you'll marry me?"

"Yes, that's the question I said yes to. Yes, Cody Dalton, I'll marry you."

He grabbed her around the waist and began to swing her in circles. "You've just made me the happiest man on the face of the earth!" Turning toward the crowd across the Square, he yelled, "Hey, everybody, she said yes!"

The two watched as Katy realizing what he was yelling, turned and yelled to those closest to her. The crowd realizing what had taken place began cheering as some of the people went into a frenzy of dancing around and clapping. The musicians began a rousing rendition of *Here Comes the Bride* as Tiny rambled down the street toward the commotion.

Cody turned back to Harley. Pulling her close, he kissed her lips.

"What say we get married right now? Right up there on that stage while most of the town's here?" asked Cody as he looked into her hazel eyes.

"Can we do that? I mean, is it legal and all."

"Yeah, kinda. It'd just be like a commitment ceremony. Wouldn't be legal until we get the license but look at it this way, we'd have two anniversaries to celebrate every year."

"Two anniversaries means two anniversary *gifts* every year," said Harley with a grin, "and I'm not talking about the kind you wrap."

"Oh woman, I like the way you think," said Cody as they headed toward the Pickin' Porch.

Cody found Reverend Lollar in the crowd and whispered into his ear. He watched as a smile broke out on the Reverend's face.

Reverend Lollar hurried up onto the stage and whispered into Elmer Shelton's ear. Elmer nodded his assent and quickly brought the music playing to a halt.

"Ladies and gentlemen," said Reverend Lollar as he motioned for everyone to quieten down, "we're gonna have a wedding!"

The crowd erupted into spontaneous applause as Cody and Harley began to climb the steps heading onto the stage.

"Hey, Cody," said Spence as he walked up behind the two. "Thought you might have need of this." He held out a folded piece of paper to Cody. "You can fill it out later."

Cody opened the paper enough he could see the heading, Application for Marriage License. He grinned.

"Guess it may be official after all," said Cody as he showed it to Harley.

"Pastor Lollar can help you take care of that part later," said Spence. "Now get on with it." Spence gave Cody a bearhug while patting him on the back. "Ma'am," he said as he tipped his hat and stepped back from the two.

Reverend Lollar began his usual dialogue for weddings and asked Cody, "Do you Dakota James Dalton, take, I'm sorry Harley, what's your whole name?"

"Uh, do we have to use my whole name?"

"Well, it is customary," replied Reverend Lollar.

Harley looked up at Cody. "Not a word out of you." She looked back at the Reverend. "It's Fifi Bridgette Mathews." Harley cocked her head and eyed Cody.

"Got something to show you," he said as he pulled the sleeve on his left arm upwards revealing his heart tattoo.

Harley gazed at the word which had obviously been freshly added. It read *Fifi*. She glanced up at Cody's eyes and back to the heart.

"How did—"

"Ran a check that first day you rode into town."

"You've known my stupid name this whole time."

"I don't think it's stupid. I kinda like it. I think it's rather sexy myself."

Harley stood looking at him for a moment.

"You never cease to amaze me." Turning back to Reverend Lollar, she said, "Okay, I guess we can get this show on the road."

"Alrighty then," said Reverend Lollar. Do you Dakota James Dalton take Fifi Bridgette Mathews as your lawfully wedded wife," he began.

Moments later Cody said "I do," as an "I do" rose right along with his from the entire crowd.

Harley quickly glanced from Cody to the crowd and back to Cody.

Reverend Lollar began "Do you Fifi Bridgette Mathews ..."

As quickly as he finished the question, Harley along with the crowd said "I do." At that moment Tiny came around the corner bellowing his assent. The bison lumbered to the steps and managed to get a front hoof on the lower step. Several men rushed over to try and steer him away but Tiny was insistent on his mission.

Gertie Mae jumped up from her seat and ran toward the bison, opening her purse as she went. Reaching the big fellow, she stuck her purse under his nose.

Whatever Tiny's thought had been, he quickly forgot it when he caught a whiff of the cannabis oil in Gertie's purse and turned to follow her.

"Good Lord almighty," whispered Cody to himself, "so that's what she's doing with that stuff." He chuckled.

Reverend Lollar continued, "I now pronounce you husband and wife. You may kiss your bride."

Cody took Harley in his arms and gently kissed her lips. She tasted sweet. He was definitely going to enjoy kissing her day and night.

The crowd stood applauding.

Pulling back from the kiss, Harley said, "This is the best Christmas anyone could ever have."

Elmer and the rest of the musicians began to play as their audience, kids and old folks alike, began to dance in celebration of another member joining their little Shady Rivers family. All was well and good.

* * *

If you enjoyed this book, please leave an honest review.

One of the best and easiest things you can do after purchasing a novel is to leave reviews. Not just one but many on different sites.

The reviews on Goodreads are seen by the super-passionate-uber-book-fans which is fantastic but your average everyday online book shopper heads to a place to actually "buy" the book like Amazon or B&N. So when you leave a review on Amazon or B&N, you are increasing the book's chance of being bought by those shoppers.

By leaving reviews on as many sites as you can find, you increase the book's *'you may also like'* algorithms. Those algorithms consider a book's popularity when making suggestions to potential consumers. Therefore, the more reviews a book has simply gives more potential for exposure.

Also, what is more enticing to you: a book with three reviews or the book with three-hundred? So help Maggie by posting reviews on numerous sites.

Thanks to all who leave reviews on Maggie's books. She appreciates them all!

COMING SOON!

More Stories in the Shady Rivers Series

Shady Rivers is a fictional small town in my home state of Alabama. With some quirky characters and a big secret, you'll come to love the town and its inhabitants. There's Colonel Bueford T. Beauregard, III, a ghost who hangs around the town's bar and Bubba, the big dude who rides a Harley and finds out the love of his life, Jonette, was a he before he became a she. Find out who or what keeps stealing apple pies from Katy's Kitchen and who saves a teacup chihuahua named Pinky.

Coming soon! Visit my website at www.maggierivers.com and sign up for my newsletter and be among the first to know when the next book in the Shady Rivers series is released.

Much love to you all!

A TRIBUTE TO MY MILITARY BROTHERS AND SISTERS

Photo Courtesy of Jennifer Wright
Carrollton, Texas

"This table is reserved to honor our missing comrades in arms. The tablecloth is white — symbolizing the purity of their motives when answering the call of duty. The single red rose, displayed in a vase, reminds us of the life of each of the missing and their loved ones and friends of these Americans who keep the faith, awaiting answers. The vase is tied with a yellow ribbon, a symbol of our continued determination to account for our missing. A pinch of salt symbolizes the tears endured by those missing and their families who seek answers. A slice of lemon on the plate reminds us of their bitter fate. The Bible represents the strength gained through faith to sustain those lost from our country, founded as one nation under God. The glass is inverted — to symbolize their inability to share this evening's toast. The chair is empty — they are missing."

Author Unknown.

Maggie is a United States Air Force Veteran who served during the Vietnam war era.

A HUGE THANK YOU!

I would like to thank you to each and every one of you who purchased my book.

You picked up my book, bought it and are right now sitting in your favorite place about to begin reading a story I created for your reading pleasure. So, yes, thank you from the bottom of my heart!

It is my hope, once you start reading this story, you absolutely cannot put it down until you reach "The End."

But really, I just appreciate the fact you've spent your hard-earned dollars purchasing one of my books. I appreciate you, my readers, whether this is the first book of mine you've purchased or your fourth or fifth.

So, yes, a gigantic thank you. I hope you enjoy it reading as much as I enjoyed writing it for you!

Love,

Maggie

P.S. I hope to meet you all in person someday!

Help Maggie Make the Best Seller Lists!

Just how can you help Maggie Rivers make the best seller lists without going bankrupt yourself? Here are a few suggestions.

1. **Post reviews to major retail sites**.

   One of the best and easiest things you can do after purchasing a novel is to leave a review. Not just one but many on different sites. The reviews on Goodreads are seen by the super-passionate-uber-book-fans which is fantastic but your average everyday online book shopper heads to a place to actually "buy" the book like Amazon or B&N. So when you leave a review on Amazon or B&N, you are increasing the book's chance of being bought by those shoppers. By leaving reviews on as many sites as you can find, you increase the book's *'you may also like'* algorithms. Those algorithms consider a book's popularity when making suggestions to potential consumers. Therefore, the more reviews a book has simply gives more potential for exposure. Also, what is more enticing to you: a book with three reviews or the book with three-hundred? So help your team by posting reviews on numerous sites.

2. **Tell others about the book.**
   Mention the books to everyone—friends, family, your social media. Word-of-mouth is huge and just talking about a title you loved can have a ripple effect. Someone picks it up because you were so enthusiastic about it. It's said that each person knows 250 people. You tell your 250, they tell their 250 who then tell their 250. And so on and so forth!

3. **Gift the book.**
   Books make wonderful gifts and you have the opportunity to have them autographed which makes them extra special! Keep several copies on hand to give for a birthday/holiday or just an "I thought of you." Authors are always grateful for extra sales!

4. **Donate a copy**.
   What do you do with your copy once it's read? If it's not something you intend to read again donate it to your local library or women's shelter. Leave a copy at your doctor's/dentist's office. If you loved the book so much you can't part with it (which we certainly hope is the case with our books), then consider buying a second copy specifically for your library. Either way ensures new readers will continue to find the title! If they like it, they'll head out to find more books by that same author.

5. **Read the book in public.**
   Or at least pretend you are. Take a physical copy and flaunt it in public places—the coffee shop, the park, the bus ride to/from work. Book lovers notice what other folks read, and someone might purchase a copy because they saw you.

6. **Recommend the title to booksellers.**
   Knowing readers are interested in a title puts it on a bookseller's radar. They might order a few copies.

7. **Place it on library hold.**
   When you don't see a book on your library's shelves, put a hold on the title through their catalog system. They'll get a copy and let you know when it arrives!

8. **Place copies on your car's dashboard.**

While you're out shopping, let your car do the advertising. Place your copies of an author's book across your car's dashboard. Back into the parking space so people walking by will see the display!

9. **Place a copy on your desk at work.**
Purchase a book stand and place it on your work desk. Showcase a different book each day. Co-workers may stop by each morning to see what's new.

Help support Maggie and together, we can make the New York Times' Best Seller list!

Thanks to all who leave reviews. I appreciate each and every one!

Maggie also writes as one of The Stiletto Girls. Check out these books with three stories in each!

BOOKS BY
The Stiletto Girls

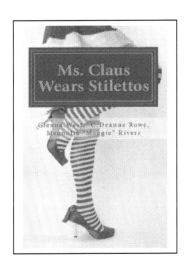

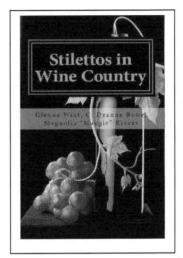

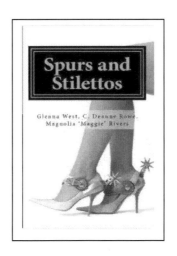

Spurs and Stilettos

Glenna West, C. Deanne Rowe,
Magnolia "Maggie" Rivers

BIOGRAPHY

MAGNOLIA "MAGGIE" RIVERS

A Southern girl born and bred, I began writing as a child, and sold my first piece of writing at the age of twenty-one.

Growing up, I spent as much of my time with books as I could. I still love that first smell of a book as you open its pages and the wonderful feel of it in your hands. Like most writers, my house is filled with books I've read countless times. I could open my own library!

I collect stilettos of all kinds and have them sitting on every available space in my office. They tend to show up in a lot of my novels as does my micro-mini teacup Chihuahua named "Mouse". Believe me though, she's no mouse. I should have named her "Killer" instead!

I write hot, sexy, sizzling romances where the hero is just what my heroine needs. He's strong and confident with broad shoulders, six-pack abs and a pleasure trail that just won't quit. His face

is more rugged than handsome, but he has a
heart of gold hidden underneath all his protective
armor.

Visit Maggie's website at:
http://www.maggierivers.com

Maggie's contact information:

P.O. Box 4601
Des Moines, IA 50305

Or by email at **maggie@maggierivers.com**

Visit Maggie's website at:
http://www.maggierivers.com

Chat with us on Facebook:
https://www.facebook.com/maggierivers-author/

To order a personally autographed copy of any of Maggie's books contact Maggie through any of the above.

If you'd like Maggie to come to your town, or skype, for a book signing, a book club meeting, a festival or any other event you might be planning, just call (515-299-5100) or email for details.

28254485R00117